Telham Park novels by
Jennifer Burton:

Princess' Journey

Christopher's Dilemma

Kenya's Song

Brian's Connection

Telham Park

KENYA'S
SONG

JENNIFER BURTON

ALEXZUS BOOKS

New York

ALEXZUS Books
244 Fifth Avenue
Suite B260
New York, NY 10001

The characters and events in this book are fictitious. Any similarity to real
persons, living or dead, is coincidental and not intended by the author.

Cover design by Rick Turylo

ISBN 978-0-9724733-4-7

Library of Congress number 2011909034

Printed in the United States of America

February 2012

For the DREAMERS . . . making two steps forward.

one

The Tuesday morning deadline for volunteers had arrived, and Nadira was still undecided. Striding through the third-floor corridor of Telham Park High School, she thumbed the papers' edges, wrestling with conflicting thoughts. *"I can pull a team of fifteen together with no problem for the "Box of Goodies" program. It's a noble cause; my civic duty and those families are homeless. What am I saying? The Youth Council, my tutoring job . . . it's impossible to do it all. But then again—"*

"Keep it moving," growled Dr. Lawson, jolting her from her reverie. "Pretend you're in school and going to class." Working hallway duty between classes seemed strange for the assistant principal *alias* comedy geek, as everything else was about this already-curious day. Entering the building had been slow due to a malfunctioning smart card reader for photo IDs. The accident on the Biltmore Parkway involving a twelve-car pileup caused a lengthy delay for faculty members commuting from the suburbs, and many had not yet arrived. The bell wasn't working properly, and students procrastinated and loitered, leaving some classrooms empty.

"Third floor done," Nadira said, checking her to-do-list as office monitor during homeroom and shot down the stairs. She avoided the "Box of Goodies" signs posted all over the first floor. *I'll just have to tell them no. Volunteering is one thing. Spearheading the campaign is another animal altogether. Looking for sponsorship, packaging the goods . . . then all the paperwork. No, no, it's too much right now. There's at least five other people who can handle it. Lindsey, Alicia, Trenton, Mack . . . but Phoenix is the one who has the experience, the personality, too. Hmm . . . but she's doing an internship on Wall Street—*"

Entering the guidance office, Nadira shouldered her way through throngs of disgruntled students waiting for program changes. The beginning of a new semester seldom arrived without frustrating challenges, long lines and bad attitudes.

"Excuse me, Mr. Burns," Nadira said, knocking quickly and opening the door to a student conference in progress. "Oooh, I'm sorry."

"It's okay. What do you need?" asked the African American counselor who was an alumnus, and favored among students.

"Four," she replied softly, handing him a program request form.

"Go ahead. You're good," he consented, and continued talking.

"Okay, you've proven yourself in Math and English, looking at these grades. You're doing great in History. So the mainstream classes are just an advanced version. I think you'll do well."

"Starting today?" asked the girl sitting before him, whose high-pitched squeal struck Nadira.

"No. This schedule goes into effect tomorrow," he explained. "Feel it out for a few days and if you're not comfortable, we can make adjustments. Understand?"

"Yes," she replied, examining the program.

Nadira cut her eyes over at the girl, matching the face to the voice. Her frazzled, boxed braids hung lamely along the side of her face, caging her features.

"But, what if the work is . . . I mean, like I don't—"

"It's only a trial, Kenya," Mr. Burns broke in, reassuring her. "Three new classes. We're not expecting miracles. If you don't earn all As, we won't be disappointed—and don't you be, either—because there's a process to change. On the other hand, if you can pull off high Cs, low Bs, we're on the way to full mainstream."

When Kenya drew her braids back, Nadira saw the healthy sum of her sweeping eyebrows guarding her tawny-brown eyes, a nicely appointed complement to her cocoa skin.

"Look," said Mr. Burns, "If you're really feeling uncomfortable with this, we can make other arrangements, but I think this is a good opportunity for you."

Kenya lowered her head again and lifted it, revived. "Okay, I'll give it a try," she said as a smile began to break.

"Now, that's what I want to hear, Kenya. Remember, it's not the skill of a man that leads to greatness . . . it's the *will* of a man."

Nadira's search for the programs intensified when she glanced at the clock. There were three stops remaining.

Curious spectators surrounded Nadira after she posted the first announcement on the "Student News" bulletin board: *AUDITIONS FOR THE SPRING TELHAM PARK IDOL SEARCH.*

"The Blackbird Violins gonna take it this year," one student said.

"Not if the New Breed Poets compete," a young man countered.

"Dile a Lakira. Que con el R&B Latino que ella canta puede ganar!" a Puerto Rican girl said to a friend, who replied in English, "Lakira, definitely!"

The rowdy, laughing track team burst in, attracting Nadira's attention as they headed toward the award's showcase. The coach was carrying a three-foot gold trophy that Christopher Murphy, the team's track star, had won at the Highland Relay Classics competition.

"Mr. Ramsey collected three hundred more cans, ya heard?" Harold asked, nudging her from behind.

"That's good," Nadira replied with an indifferent air. Catching his glance, the memory of the past weekend came rushing back, reminding her of what had transpired.

"Still working with me on the food drive?"

Nadira replied with a long, annoying sigh.

Harold was more attractive than he gave himself credit for, and there was no denying his tall, knightly physique. It was also no secret that he adored Nadira—for everything she represented—dark elegance, her shapely lean body, long black hair and all.

"Is that a no?"

The food drive was Mr. Ramsey's brainchild, a physical education teacher and descendent of the Cherokee Indians, whose family lived in the Midwestern region. Harold had volunteered to spearhead the committee to help the people who had been misplaced following the recent hurricane.

"I always keep my promise," Nadira said above the noise in the bustling hallway. "What'd you think, I was gonna let the people starve?"

Harold smiled generously, relieved, and then whispered, "Still mad at me? You know I didn't—"

"Forget about it," she said tersely, cutting him off.

He drove his hand into his pocket and leaned into her. "For real . . . I'm sorry."

Nadira glanced back shrewdly at his pleading eyes giving him no indication that his apology was accepted. The young man was guilty, and she wanted him to know it, but he wasn't the only one exhibiting somewhat erratic behavior these days. They were all in a state of flux over Deshon, their friend and native of Telham Park. The time had come for him to meet the inevitable consequences for his recent gang activity. They were relieved, however, that the boot camp sentence he received was his one last opportunity to get it right—in his head and heart—before finding a permanent home in an adult correctional facility. They were unsure, however, that Deshon could survive ninety days of confinement and hard labor.

Recalling the dreadful departure was painful. The whole group of them—Nadira, Harold, Christopher, Maverick, Cicely, Alonzo, Jerome and Bianca—gathered together in front of Deshon's house on Saturday to say goodbye. It was cold and damp outside, and they warmed themselves with quivering remembrances of past events, already feeling his absence.

Christopher wanted to be the last one to see him. He caught the childlike panic that peeps out of a man in Deshon's face as he entered the basement. His coffee-brown eyes revealed that he was scared, and without his smile there were no familiar dimples. Stripped of all of his "bling-bling" and trendy gear—wearing a pair of jeans and a simple button-down shirt—Deshon resembled a young boy.

"What's good, yo, how you feelin'?" Christopher asked.

"I'm good."

The basement was immaculate; every item was meticulously arranged. Two open drawers were all Deshon had completed on the entertainment/office center he'd recently began working on. Just like him—unfinished, imperfect, a work interrupted.

"What color you gonna paint it?" Christopher asked, examining the birch melamine.

"Thinkin' about doin' it in that high-gloss black."

"That'll work."

"I'ma leave it down here."

"You buildin' it as one piece or what?"

"I want to do it separately. Easier to move that way."

"Okay." Amid the brief silence, images of Deshon working industriously flashed through Christopher's mind.

"I got my boys lookin' out for you," Deshon uttered, moving his duffel bag toward the door.

"The Eastern Thugs ain't tryin' to come near me. That's done."

"I don't trust 'em, yo."

"I heard some talk about the Thugs callin' a truce."

"Hope so . . . if they know what I know."

"You need to let that go, man. The world is bigger than this. You know how close you came to—"

Hearing Deshon's father coming down the stairs brought the conversation to a halt. Facing the inevitable, they shook hands and embraced, each of them bending their nerves to keep their emotions in check.

"You're gonna be alright," encouraged Christopher.

"Ay . . . gotta adjust. You know me."

"Yeah, that's what scares me."

Christopher threw several jabs to Deshon's chest to lighten the mood. Deshon feigned distress in his usual way, but the moment Mr. Taylor appeared, their faces stiffened.

"Let's get out of here," Christopher ordered, parting the group outside.

This was a defining moment, alerting them all to their infallibility, which, if they weren't careful, could lurk like an invisible pit, awaiting their disobedience.

"McCuller's got the triple burger special today," Jerome said, breaking the silence.

"I ain't had nothin' all day," Maverick realized, patting his stomach. His slender face was hidden underneath his cap.

"Tight," Alonzo agreed, lighting up a cigarette. Alonzo was a black-haired, black-eyed young man with Italian and Spanish blood. His glossy eyes never released a tear.

"Feels like somebody died," said Nadira.

"I know, it does, right?" Bianca agreed. She was an olive-skinned Brazilian beauty with a smooth, finished face and pretty black hair.

"Kinda sorta does," Maverick realized, lowering his chin into his turtleneck.

"Deshon ain't dead, yo!" Alonzo grumbled, annoyed. "Just temporarily out of service."

BENEATH THE thumping music at McCuller's restaurant, they picked over their food while making feeble attempts at conversation. Ironically, the popular thug anthem was one of Deshon's favorites and had played for the third time.

Alonzo walked to the jukebox, snapping his fingers to the rhythm of the beat. Holding to a two-step, he threw his hands up in the air, made a complete 360 and leaned back . . . to the beat . . . and leaned back . . . to the beat. Now owning the rhythm and feeling at one with it, he bent his muscular body low, fingers almost touching the floor . . . to the beat. Coming up straight, he opened his arms wide like he was flying . . . to the beat . . . then stretched his arms forward, one at a time, like he was swimming . . . to the beat. Moving free and easy, he forgot the others in the room were watching him, and stayed true to his groove . . . to the beat. No one had ever recalled Alonzo dancing, until now.

Christopher stared at the ceiling, and his look of intensity roused the others.

"What's on your mind?" Maverick asked.

Christopher's eyes rolled over to him with a distant gaze. "Could've finished buildin' that wall unit."

"You talkin' about Deshon."

"Had skills, yo," said Alonzo, who had returned to his seat.

"Building," said Christopher. "It's what we all need to be doin'."

"Whatchu mean?" Maverick asked.

"I told him he was moving too fast . . . and look at this," Alonzo said.

"Some people gotta feel the fire to know it's hot," Christopher added. "Seein' the flames ain't good enough for some."

A LOW, hanging sky pulled the dreary day into evening. Still together, the group arrived at the school track oval.

"Tomorrow's another day," Christopher said. Well-built and handsome, he exhibited the cool charm of a prince and kept his wits about him. Christopher looked a bit older than the rest, now that he was growing a goatee. And he was as dedicated to winning a school championship as he was to the history books that he routinely devoured.

They watched him moving inside the field beginning with an even, steady jog. Wearing his thermal sweat suit, he built up his stride and in no time increased his speed. Awed, they watched him circling the track with fierce determination.

"That's my man," praised Alonzo.

"Can't nobody touch 'em," said Harold. "He's gonna put Telham Park High on the map, I'm tellin' you."

Their fingers clutched the fence wires, sharing in the thrill of his athletic, lean legs seamlessly slicing through the open air.

"Lightning's hurtin', yo," said Maverick, calling him by his nickname. "I can feel it."

On that note, everyone fell silent, and the group decided to leave the track and head to the Starview Houses, where Harold lived, only four blocks away.

"We gonna hit the game room now," said Alonzo, who had just closed a call on his cell phone. "Jason and Lexis are waiting for me. They're drag-racing down by Randall's."

"I'm going, too," said Maverick.

"Hey, I got the food drive stuff upstairs," Harold said to Nadira. "I can give it to you now."

"We can do that later," Nadira answered. "We need to organize everything strategically, and I'm not feeling it—"

"Might as well do it now," Harold broke in. "You're here, it's early, and I'll walk you back later."

"I'm hookin' up with Leron and Sasha, so go ahead," said Bianca.

Finally Nadira agreed, and everyone else went their separate ways.

NADIRA appreciated the understated elegance of the Singleton's living room. White walls served as a striking background to statues of Egyptian deities and distinctive, traditional African masks. She sat down sideways, inspecting the African Thunder Gods aligned on the bookshelves as she removed her coat.

"You want something to drink?" Harold asked, going into the kitchen.

"Nope, I'm good."

"I would ask you if you wanted something to eat, but I know you're not hungry."

"How you know that?"

" 'Cause we just ate," he said, gazing awkwardly at her.

"I'm jokin', stupid. But I really didn't eat much. Appetite's not that uh—" A black-and-white mask on lower shelf caught her attention. "I've never seen this one."

"Oh yeah, it's new," Harold said, returning with a bottle of water. "My father bought it for my mother's birthday."

"This is real nice," Nadira commented, running her finger along the contour of its edges.

"It's a Kuba mask . . . some kind of mythological character. Look," he said, pointing his eyes toward the canvas. "She's trying to paint it."

Doing a double-take, Nadira stood amazed; it was an uncanny resemblance. Watching her, Harold eased his way closer to her and slid his arm around her waist. Then he lowered his head into the valley of her neck, trying to kiss her. Nadira resisted his warm advances and returned to the couch.

Harold went into his room and returned with several newspaper articles highlighting the tragic events in Nebraska.

"That hurricane was angry," Nadira said, perusing the pictures.

"Wiped out a lot of people," said Harold. "Here, this is draft of the flyer. I'm thinking about some drop sites at laundromats, supermarkets—"

"This time tomorrow Deshon's gonna be in jail," Nadira said absently.

"It's not as bad as prison," he said, following her train of thought. "He'll be alright." Harold leaned back, absorbing the music, and put his arm around Nadira. Assured that they were lost together on Cupid's rooftop, shot there by a mystical golden arrow, he pulled her closer. Nadira rested her head on his shoulder with volleying thoughts, from fear of falling short of all her responsibilities, to missing her friend Princess, to imagining Deshon in boot camp.

Soft kisses lightly tapped her forehead, but when his strong hand turned her face toward his, Nadira resisted, partitioning them with her hand. Ignoring her, he drove his lips toward hers. Quickly she turned and caused him to miss his aim, and with that he proceeded with kisses along her cheek and down her neck.

Allowing herself only a brief moment of his tantalizing pleasure, she recanted softly, "C'mon, it's time to go."

"You just got here," he said, returning to their comfortable embrace.

"I know, but it's getting warm in here, c'mon."

Harold didn't respond. Nor did he stop kissing her. When she tried to pull away, he forced her back with such strength their bodies fell together, horizontally.

"Stop that. Hey . . . I'm not playin'. Stop!"

As he released her and they pulled themselves forward, for the briefest of moments she wanted to submit to him . . . but that look in his eyes cautioned her. "Let's go," she said again and stood up to gather her things.

They stepped around each other, fanning their libidos as if nothing had happened. When Nadira reached for the doorknob, Harold took hold of her wrist, turned her toward him and kissed her again. This time he didn't miss and she didn't resist.

In the heat of the moment, her backpack dropped to the floor as he pressed himself against her, and his hands began to roam below her waist.

"Don't do that!" she objected, coming to her senses.

Harold held her tighter, working his way into another kiss.

"C'mon, stop!" she demanded, wiggling and winding, trying to escape his tight grip on her.

Nothing deterred him.

"Get away from me!" she urged, squirming and throwing punches to his back. Finally, she pinched the flesh of his neck between her fingers and twisted it until he felt the sting.

"I'm sorry," he apologized, backing away.

She narrowed her eyes, shaming him, as he came back to himself. Embarrassed that he had lost control, he picked her bag up off the floor and headed out the door. She said only four words to him after that. "Thanks for the walk."

"Auditions already?" piped a girl named Meisha, redirecting Nadira's thoughts back to the present. The crowd had swelled exponentially in a very short time, and Harold had been distracted with his friends.

"Jordan Nichols for Vice President. Nichols for Vice President," crooned the African American squeezing his way through the crowd. The strong featured, brown-haired teenager was admired by his peers—above and beyond his attractiveness and toned physique—for his dedication to excellence. He was the school's leading debater, held the highest grade point average in the eleventh grade, and led several civic activities around the city.

"Sign my petition, please," he asked, offering a clipboard to Nadira.

"Early, aren't you?" she asked, looking up into his dark eyes through his Browline frames. "Elections don't begin until the fall."

"I'm trying to get a jump on things, feel me . . . get my supporters now. Ay, I didn't see your name on the list for the campaign."

"I'm still thinking about it," Nadira told him as she walked. "So talk to me. Why should I vote for you?"

"I got major plans. I want to start a school bank—like a credit union—get an entrepreneurship program going, buy new computers and I want to um . . . create more sports teams."

"What else you got?"

"Ay, you lookin' at a scholar, a gentleman . . . voice of the people."

"Okay, now you're speakin' my language."

two

Kenya shifted nervously in her chair and peered optimistically at her new program. *Three classes now, and by senior year I could apply to college. Mommy will hit the roof! I could be the first one in the family to go . . . and graduate.*

Of the twelve students enrolled in math class, Jeff Paggart made ten who were present today. He entered the room hitting the walls with his fist, mumbling fiercely. Ruggedly handsome, he was extremely popular at school but tried to keep his status a secret. Growing tired of dodging and hiding or covering the glass window on the door, he came to class late every day so the mainstream girls wouldn't know he was in Special Education.

It seemed odd for Kenya to find herself separating from students that she had been in classes with for years. Some were slow to learn, had behavioral difficulties, problems with speech patterns, or were physically challenged. Some didn't walk at all—like Sheronda. Ms. Rudby, the handicap assistant, wheeled her into class every day.

"They changed my schedule," Kenya whispered, leaning into Camilla who was seated to her left.

Camilla looked curiously at Kenya, who was displaying her program. "To what?"

"Mainstream. I've got three new classes, see?"

Camilla's head snapped up in surprise, now understanding. "Kenya's going to mainstream," she blurted out.

"Starting tomorrow," Mr. Morton said, turning with an appreciative nod.

"Good!" Gary said sarcastically.

"That's right, good!" Kenya responded. "Now I can get away from you." She never took any of them seriously, understanding how difficult it was to adjust to people transitioning in and out of their lives so frequently.

Completing the math assignment with exceptional ease brought a smile to Kenya's face as she appreciated the decision the school made to advance her. Now, feeling a song in her head, she flipped to the back of her notebook and began penning the words:

"On this day
I will remember
The feeling, the gladness
The jitters, the sadness

On this day
I will remember
The hoping, the clinging,
The wanting, the changing

On this day
I will remember—"

The words came as quickly to her as she could write them down, while simultaneously staying abreast of the lesson. In between, a million thoughts consumed her—the past, present and the much-anticipated future.

"*ONE HUNDRED twenty-two . . . one hundred twenty-three . . . one hundred twenty-four . . . one hundred twenty-five*," Kenya counted in her head, enduring the chilly wind on her way home from school. The cracked sidewalk curving around the corner of Lott Street, which landmarked the border of the "ville"—short for Bedville— was exactly one hundred seventy-seven steps from her front door. Kenya's one-way street had slowly become a hotbed of typical urban disturbances. Each of the old detached dwellings stood as markedly divided as the lives that occupied them.

"What up?" Conway greeted, pedaling by on a worn 10-speed bicycle. The man in his 60s, had recently been a squatter of the only church on the block and was forced to move out. The only thing left of Bedville Baptist was its shell and the bright white letters bearing its name.

"Hey," was Kenya's reply as she continued counting in her head. "*One hundred fifty-two . . . three . . . four . . . five . . .*"

Up ahead, she could see her older brother Chad approaching the house from the opposite direction. Slender and tall, donning shoulder-length dreads, he walked with the stride of a king, never in a hurry. At nineteen—after dropping out of high school with six months left to go—Chad had lost his motivation and began drifting. One day he was rapping, the next day he was claiming a pursuit in journalism or starting a business, but he lacked the discipline necessary to carry out any of his ideas.

"Where are you coming from?" Kenya asked, opening the thin metal gate.

"Don't matter," he answered, trailing her. "It's where I'm goin'."

"Yeah, okay."

The pungent aroma of barbecued chicken met them at the door. "Do something about this, Chad," Kenya pointed, careful not to touch the wires protruding from the wall. "Mommy's been asking you forever."

"I look like the landlord to you?"

"Until the real one gets here, yeah. Look how they're sticking out. Somebody can get—"

"Ayyy . . . there's my chocolate chip yong yongs." Mali and Morocco, Kenya's younger brothers, three and five respectively, suddenly charged into her.

"Give me some sugar!" she happily exclaimed. After embracing both with loving kisses, she swept one up in her arms while the other tugged at her legs and dragged her into the kitchen.

"Guess what, Mommy?"

Observing the light in Kenya's face, her curious mother put down her scissors abruptly. "What happened?"

"They changed my schedule today. They're giving me mainstream classes. Look."

"That's where you should have been all the time," Chad remarked, lifting the lids of the cooking pots, previewing dinner. "Always tryin' to tell us we stupid. I told you that was crap!"

"Thank God," Ms. Robinson sighed gratefully, reading the program. "I knew you were coming out of there. I knew it!"

"You shouldn't have let her go there in the first place."

Ms. Robinson ignored Chad's comments, refusing to be pulled into his negative tirade, and beamed in approval. She was a shade lighter than Kenya, small and shapely, bowlegged, and cute. With a T-shirt and jeans on, she was often asked if she were Chad's girlfriend. In church on Sundays, she was the best-looking woman in the choir, her peachy complexion glowing. And when she opened her mouth to sing, her soulful voice charged the atmosphere.

"Thank you, Jesus, thank you, Lord!" she hailed.

"Ain't no big deal. Boobie shoulda been out of there," remarked Chad.

Ms. Robinson's smile turned cold, and her eyes swept over him. "Am I going to have to hear this for the rest of my life, Mr. Perfect? Who knows? Maybe this was all for the best."

"What? For Boobie to be labeled?"

"Kenya needed some extra attention, that's all. She got the help she needed, and now she's moving on. It's better than what you're doing."

"One thing don't have nothin' to do with the other," argued Chad.

"Yes, it does. Look in the mirror and check on yourself and then you can criticize others."

The two of them rarely saw eye to eye on things, almost like siblings. Unlike the rest of them, Chad had been raised with his paternal grandmother until the age of seven. His mother had prayed that Chad would not inherit the characteristics of his recalcitrant, unrestrained renegade of a father. Yet with every year, the signs of his likeness were becoming more evident.

Though he wouldn't admit it, Chad resented his poverty and had a way of aiming his dismay toward his mother. He disliked the small, shabby house they lived in, the second-hand or discounted clothes they wore, and the lack of cultural exposure, technology, and other advantages of the twenty-first century.

Ms. Robinson never liked to hear the truth, especially when it highlighted the main areas in her life: four demanding children, single motherhood, deprived of a promising opera career, and economic instability right on the verge of reaching her thirty-eighth birthday.

"Forget him, Mommy," Kenya said, dismissing his presence.

"Aunt Sophie's gonna be so proud of you."

"I'll tell her on Thursday."

AFTER DINNER, Kenya retreated to her room upstairs. The seven-by-seven space had formerly been a walk-in storage closet in the attic, and there was only room for a twin-size bed and a small dresser with a mirror attached. The flea market special housed all her meager belongings, including her book of songs. Sitting on her bed, she opened the newspaper to read her horoscope:

Virgo: Today, your lunar energy ignites a passion in you that others will begin to notice. New changes in your career will lead you on an accelerated track. Move forward fearlessly and prepare for a safe landing.

Excited, Kenya reached underneath her mattress and pulled out her beige sweater—the one she liked best. *I can match this up with my black jeans. Yeah, but they're old. No, maybe it'll look better with my long jean skirt. No! But I don't have any nice shoes to wear with it.*

Thinking, Kenya opened the bottom drawer of the dresser and pulled out a tin cookie can full of change. She remembered her balance, but counted the coins anyway. Seventeen dollars and eight cents was all she had. *If I could catch a yellow tag sale at the thrift store, I could buy two more pair of vintage jeans. Yeah, but some of their styles are yuk!!!*

Kenya would have liked to have a makeover, go to school with some new clothes, get her hair done, and buy a new coat and bag, but she quickly dismissed the idea. Not for one moment would she ever think of pressuring her mother to do more than she could financially handle. Their meals were hot, the roof over their heads was solid, and her dream she visited every night—a beautiful house, plenty of money, cars and travel—was going to come true for them . . . one of these days.

three

Nadira gathered her long braids together and tied them in a rubber band, contemplating her ideas about the after-school youth council meeting. She shut her locker door and rushed out to the gym floor for the attendance lineup.

Kenya primped in the mirror, evaluating her appearance, and hummed nervously, as she was one of the last girls out.

Nadira did a double take, recognizing the bashful girl from the guidance office as she walked by her. With her braids styled differently—only two this time—she didn't appear as drab. Her features were more pronounced and her skin looked satiny smooth.

A stream of afternoon sunshine lit up one side of the gym when Mr. Braithwaite opened the partition that separated the boys' side from the girls. He called Ms. Duncan's attention away from them.

In their brief idle moment, a group of boys rushed over to the opening to view the irresistible display of girls. They squeezed closely together, see-sawing their necks and tiptoeing above each other's heads to get a glimpse of them stretching, bending and exercising their limbs.

"Yeah, that's nice right there," Dexter Madison said, pointing to a busty, full-figured young girl.

"She's too short," said one of the boys.

"If everything else is working, don't matter," Dexter uttered.

"That's the flavor right there, yo," Jameel remarked, looking at a sexy, slender yellowish-brown stunner.

"Yeah, well, none of them look as good as Princess," observed Christopher.

"She don't count," said Marcus. " 'Cause she ain't here."

"Watch yourself, dude."

Pointing and proposing, the boys became riled up in competition on justifying their preferences.

"Tone it down, yo," Julio reminded them when they became too loud. A Dominican girl with searing green eyes and long, sandy-brown hair attracted him. "Mira, presiosa."

"Oooh, como esta mom-me-tha," teased Rasta Ricky, altering accents from his Jamaican origin.

"What kind of spanglish is that?" asked Malik.

"Look at that one right there, second row, now move down to the middle," Zachary pointed. "The one with the big legs and the honeydew melons. I can smell her perfume from here."

"Control yourself," said Jameel.

Leron Tatum never appeared anxious for any girl. As one of the most handsome young men in Telham Park High School—tall with an athletic build, dark-featured, tan-skinned and a swamp of curly hair he wore in a bushy tail—he didn't have to. Massaging his hairy chin, he was well-focused on his subject. "Look down that middle row . . . toward the back . . . black shorts, white shirt. I could work with that."

They all discovered a girl that no one had noticed before.

"Watch her when she turns around . . . perfect proportion."

"She packin' a little su um, su um," agreed Harold.

"Yo, she Special Ed," a guy named Marcus realized. "I saw her in the, ah—"

"Not any more," Jameel corrected. "She's in seventh period math with me."

"What's the difference? That's where she came from."

"Yeah, 'cause she was in the class with my brother Jakequon," said Malik. "I've seen her there before."

"Don't matter," Leron said. "The slower the better. 'Cause that right there . . . with that body . . . worth gettin' into some extracurricular activity with."

"You would get with that?" Zachary asked, frowning with curiosity.

"That's right."

"Look aiight from here, but she ain't no—"

"Look, you take that body," Leron said cutting Jameel off. "And you can go anywhere with that. Okay, right now she's lookin' a li'l shy, but I can break her out of that. And she's a little cute. I'm telling you, watch out for them average girls or dem girls y'all think ain't all of that, 'cause yo . . . they grow into stars. See, the girls that are fine now, psss . . . they in their glory days, I'm tellin' you."

"Where you come up with that theory?" Christopher queried.

"Experience. Look, I've been following my brother since I was little. He's what . . . ten years older than me. I watched him comin' up with some of the hottest, I'm talkin' pretty . . . the kind of girls you be droolin' over. I see them now . . . in their late twenties. Girlz is hurtin' yo: got babies runnin' after them, big round guts hanging over their jeans, lookin' all tired. And then the ones I remember seein' . . . who was like average. I'm tellin' you . . . they bad!"

"So what you sayin' is these are your best days," said Zachary.

Leron faked a backhand and Zachary ducked, bringing on more laughter.

"Well, that's what you said. These are the glory days for the fine girls, so I assume the same rule applies to you."

"Don't assume, Jack! I'm the exception to da rule, yo. You got eyes, don't you?" Leron returned his hand to his chin and resumed his gaze on the subject. "That's the one right there."

"You serious about that?" Christopher asked, thinking of his friend Deshon at that moment.

"As serious as I am about gettin' that bike," he replied mildly, with the confidence of a champion.

"That Fury Base joint?"

"Nah, the Kawasaki Classic LT."

"I feel you, but you know your Pops is not gonna let you have it," Christopher said, jolting his ambition.

"Psss . . . I'll take care of him," Leron recoiled. "Eighteen's around the corner."

"Yeah, right," Christopher chuckled, well knowing how strict Leron's father was.

"But what makes you think she's gonna bite?" Marcus asked.

"This face, this body," he boasted, looking over himself. "Who wouldn't?"

"Ten dollars if you don't," muttered one of them.

"Who said that?" Leron asked.

Zachary stepped away from the crowd, the shortest of them all. "I said it."

"I say it, too," Marcus added.

"Me, too," Jameel said, joining in the circle.

"Anybody else?" Leron asked, looking over his shoulder to the right and then to the left.

"Me," said Malik.

"Yeah, *mon*," said Rasta Ricky. He was game as well.

Christopher and Harold walked away; unimpressed by the unconscionable challenge the group had conjured.

"Iight," Leron said. "When I get to swimmin', I'm collecting fifty dollaz, cuz shorty's mine."

"And when you find yourself in the desert you gotta pay us fifty," Malik added.

"Bet." Leron replied, sealing the challenge.

KENYA ROTATED into the serving position, anxious to take advantage of her debut in the volleyball game. Seven to six, their team down, was the score. Using the underhand serve technique, her right arm swung back, then forward, transferring her body weight to bring more power. Her strong fist sent the ball flying hard and fast to the middle of the opposite team's court. Bouncing off clumsy, fumbling hands, the ball hit the floor. Her team applauded vigorously, bringing them to an even score.

Next, Kenya used the overhand serve, giving the ball a higher trajectory. Cutting the wind fast and hard, a girl in the first row attempted the return, but it bounced off the tips of her fingers, fell toward the middle, and when the next girl behind her tried to pick it up with a clenched-fist clasp and take it over, the ball hit the net. The girls applauded louder. By the end of class, Kenya's team had won, leading by six points.

"We gonna kill 'em tomorrow," said Nadira, throwing her arm around Kenya as they entered the locker room.

Kenya's began cheerfully humming as she sat down and started to untie her sneakers, recalling her performance. Winning the game for the team was emotionally uplifting, inspiring a song that flowed naturally out of her:

> *"In all the years*
> *I searched for you*
> *There you were*
> *Right next to me*
> *Shielding the storms*
> *The rain, fire and flames*
> *We were good friends"*

The locker room acoustics amplified her lilting voice and heartened the dull atmosphere. She felt alive inside, empowered, as the extraordinary sound sprang from her vocal treasure.

Kenya opened the locker, patting the moisture around her temples. Evaluating her features in the mirror—this time approving of her image—she saw the face of a winner. And it tickled her into another verse:

"During the hard
And lonely times
I saw you
Were lonely too

And then we laughed
We cried
We shared all our dreams
And we're now one"

Well into the depths of her song, against the sound of clanging locker doors, Kenya closed her eyes, and with her head leaned back, she belted out a generous dose of her amazing vocals:

"And when tomorrow comes
I know you'll be
There for me—"

Kenya jumped back, startled when she opened her eyes to an audience of girls. "Oh God, y'all scared me!"

"That's really your voice," said Nadira, fixing an incredulous gaze upon her.

"You heard me?"

"We all heard you," one girl said, an ear-to-ear smile on her face.

"How could we not?" another girl blurted out.

"I thought it was coming from somebody's iPod," Nadira said.

"But then we didn't hear any music," one of the other girls rejoined.

"I've never heard singing like that before," a sassy, petite girl chimed in. "Not live, anyway."

The other girl, big and buxom, looked at Kenya as if she had three eyes. "My God!"

"C'mon, don't stop now. Finish the song?" Nadira requested eagerly.

Kenya smiled, unable to look them in their eyes, and began fumbling with her things inside the locker.

"Oh, c'mon, don't tell me you're shy," Nadira teased, holding her head between her hands.

The bigger girl shook her head and walked away. "Y'all heard her. It's the real thing," she blasted out to others in the locker room.

"No seriously, you ever sang in front of anyone before?" asked Nadira.

"Yeah."

"Where?"

"Church."

"Oooooh!" Nadira put her hands together, praise-style. "You need to sing in the talent search! You would blow—them—away!"

Kenya chuckled, finding comedy in Nadira's enthusiasm.

"I'm dead serious! You could win!"

"I gotta cousin that can *sang*," another girl jumped in, "but she don't sound nothin' like that."

The girls gazed admirably at Kenya and returned to their lockers one by one, leaving Nadira alone with her.

"The audition is the week after next. That's, what . . . twelve, fourteen days away. All you have to do is—"

"No," Kenya declined, still chuckling. "I don't think so."

"You'll only be singing in front of a few people—Ms. Kaplan and the other students trying out. Why not?"

Kenya considered the possibility for a split-second and then said, "No, I . . . I couldn't do that."

"Are you crazy . . . with a voice like that?"

Kenya appreciated the compliment, tossing her another grin.

"Okay, you scared? Nervous? What?" Nadira was now standing closer to Kenya, her eyes almost pleading.

"No, it's not that, but . . . nobody knows me."

"Well I tell you one thing, when you open up your mouth . . . everybody's gonna know who you are . . . and be glad about it, too. I mean, so what if people don't know you now? That's the point."

"There's other students here who can sing. I hear them."

"So what?" Competition is good, but c'mon . . . you know as well as I do that you got a gazillion-dollar sound!"

They laughed as a tacit acknowledgement to the truth.

Nadira looked at Kenya, thinking. "Is that why you have such a high-pitched voice? Cause you can sing?"

"I don't know, I guess," Kenya shrugged.

The bell rang, suddenly catching both of them off guard.

"I gotta go," said Nadira, rushing off to her locker. "We'll finish this tomorrow. Think about it. Hard!"

"Okay."

four

Heavy rain poured over Telham Park on Thursday evening. Running from the bus stop to the door of the Crestfield House, Kenya narrowly escaped getting drenched. Two nights a week she volunteered in the senior citizen home to—among other things—take care of Aunt Sophie, the vibrant 89-year-old woman who had become her friend.

Inside the reception area, decorated with marble floors, warm pastel walls and receding lights, a beautiful fire burned. Kenya detected the smell of meatloaf coming from the dining room as she signed in at the desk and hummed quietly to the soft music overhead. Drawn momentarily to the fireplace, it took her back to the special day two years ago when she'd first met Aunt Sophie.

William Harvey, the 19-year-old visiting minister, was in rare form that Sunday morning, delivering a profound message on Christian values for young adults. In an emotional, spiritual outburst the congregation hailed praises and wept to the ONE above after the rendition of songs led by Kenya and the youth choir. A record number of young people came forward and accepted Christ that afternoon while Kenya enhanced his greeting with soothing melodies on the piano.

A well-dressed, elderly woman seated in a wheelchair stalled the flow of traffic as the young adult choir filed down the aisle of the church. Instinctively, Kenya rolled the woman out of the way behind the back pew, awaiting the assistance of one of the ushers. The elderly lady nodded her head thankfully and pointed to the ladies' room.

"You have to use the bathroom?" Kenya asked.

"No. What's your name, honey?"

"Kenya."

"Kenya, I'm Sophia. Sophie Nichols. Um, Sandy's in there. I don't think she's feeling too well."

"Sister Miller, the usher?"

"Yes. Would you go in there and check on her?"

Kenya did as she asked, then quickly alerted several adults when she found the woman on the floor in one of the stalls, unconscious. Paramedics were called and were able to revive her and stabilize her blood pressure and then rushed her to the hospital. Kenya remained with the woman, whom she referred to as Ms. Sophie, serving her dinner while she waited for the church van to escort her home.

"Thank you, young lady," Ms. Sophie said, as she entered the vehicle.

Underneath her hat, Kenya could see the fatigue in Ms. Sophie's eyes, a translucent brown color that, set against her delicate, light skin, made her look almost white.

"You're welcome . . . and I'm sorry about your friend."

"She'll be alright, thank God. I'll see you next week."

Kenya attended the church dinner next week, but Ms. Sophie wasn't there. While she and her friends were eating, an usher handed Kenya a gift-wrapped box. Inside was a beautiful white silk blouse. The card read: Angels sometimes come disguised as strangers. What a pleasure to make your acquaintance. Sophie.

Kenya, in turn, bought her a beautiful Thank-You card. When that next Sunday had arrived, Kenya and Sophie Nichols had become not only friends, but "Ms. Sophie" was now referred to as "Aunt Sophie."

Feeling warmed by her memories, Kenya was ready to begin her duties when Imani, who worked with her, rushed in, huffing and puffing. She was never late, but always arrived at the last minute.

"I'm gonna end this *today*!" she snapped.

"What happened?"

"I'll tell you later, but I'm out of there!"

Possessing a Castilian-brown complexion, Imani lived up to her exotic name. She had a pretty face with glistening eyes, a sexy smile, and a well-endowed, shapely figure. After losing her mother at a young age, she had been bounced from relative to relative. Later, she moved into a string of foster homes and got caught up in the whimsical forces of life's unfair and unexplained circumstances.

Aunt Sophie was sitting in the spacious sunroom where she loved to read. Kenya stood in the doorway watching her as she caressed the silver key that hung around her neck.

"Knocka, knocka. Look, what I bought for you."

The twice-widowed gentlewoman jerked forward, closed her book and removed her glasses. Kenya pulled out two bags of freshly washed grapes—one green bunch, one red.

"Now that's a good girl," Aunt Sophie said as she reached out.

"Easy now. You should only have a few at a time," Kenya warned, watching her hungry eyes. "You can save the rest for tomorrow."

"What's it gonna do, kill me?" she uttered. "Nu uh baby, life is for the living."

"C'mon now, the sugar's not good for your pressure."

"Can't hang around here forever."

"Stop talking like that."

Imani entered the room, offering Aunt Sophie a cold drink.

"Good, now I can tell y'all together," Kenya said. "Something happened to me this week that you would not believe."

"Whatever it is . . . gonna be good for you."

"How do you know?" Kenya said, stroking Aunt Sophie's soft, silky hair. "I could be talking about something bad."

"But you're not, so spill it, child. Time is precious. You've been singing to somebody?"

"Nope. Well, yes, but that's not it." Kenya walked around the chair and squatted on the floor. "All those writing lessons you gave me are starting—to—pay—off!"

"How's that?"

"They put me into mainstream. Well . . . not all the way, but now I have three mainstream classes."

Aunt Sophie smacked her lips as she sampled the green grapes for sweetness. Satisfied, she soon broke into a smile. "Didn't I tell you?"

"You sure did," Kenya giggled, teasing at her ankle.

"Listen to the old lady. You have to believe in that which you desire, my dear, and the universe will oblige."

"You're still in Special Ed," Imani reminded her.

"Don't be so quick to discount progress, young lady," Aunt Sophie said. "All things in time."

"Well I'm just sayin'. They still got you—"

"Look at all these new books they gave me," Kenya presented, cutting her off.

"Good for you. 'Cause you got nothing else to do with your time."

"True."

"Huh . . . I gotta lot of things to do with my time," mumbled Imani.

"You grow up too quick, you get robbed," Aunt Sophie remarked.

Imani paused briefly, pondering her words. "What do you mean?"

"You know what I'm talking about."

Kenya and Imani shot curious glances at each other. "We have to tour the second floor with afternoon snacks," said Imani, signaling a needed confrontation with Kenya.

"I'll be back shortly, Aunt Sophie."

"Um huh."

There was traffic in the corridors, and each time they had to stop to speak to someone, Imani grew more frustrated.

"So what happened?"

"I was out with Mike, right, and I came in like . . . twenty minutes late, and Sandy was having a fit."

"Because you were twenty minutes late?"

"Okay, more like forty or forty-five minutes, but she said it was an hour. Anyway, it wasn't a big deal. She started yellin' and screamin', gettin' all up in my face. You don't know . . . I felt like smackin' her. But I just went to my room and I slammed that door so hard—"

"Hi, Ms. Martin," Kenya interrupted, cutting Imani off.

"Hello girls. How's it going?"

"Good," they chorused, smiling and waiting until Ms. Martin was out of earshot.

"So I started taking off my clothes," Imani quickly continued. "Soon as I pulled my pants down, she busted in the door and saw it."

"Saw what?"

Imani pulled Kenya into the vending machine room. "I'ma get a soda." After she inserted the change and pressed the button of her preference, she turned around and peeled her jeans back from her waist to reveal the right side of her buttocks. Tattooed into her skin was a multicolored butterfly.

Kenya gasped. "You got inked! Did it hurt?"

The soda thumped as it dropped down in the receiving bucket.

"Not really. I had asked her for the money to get one, and she gonna tell me no. She said I would have to wait till I turn eighteen. That's crazy."

"But where did you—"

"Mike paid for it, but she don't know about him." Imani picked up the soda and popped open the top.

"Let me see it again." This time Kenya looked closer, reading the letters. "You tattooed his name on you?"

"That's my man."

"No wonder she was mad."

"And she talkin' about 'you're on punishment until further notice.' I told her I don't have to stay here."

"And where you goin'?" Kenya probed.

"I can move in with Mike."

"What!"

"Yep, he got the hook up with the manager at the Hip-Hop Sub Shop, and I can get a job there."

"Okay getting a job is good, but—"

"In her house it's not, 'cause she said I don't need to be workin' when I'm only making C's in school. So if I leave, even if I have to go back to the group home, it's cool. At least I can work . . . and get privileges. Then she's gonna tell me, for disobeying her, I'm gonna have to come straight home after school every day and on the weekend I'll have to baby-sit her kids. I'll do a disappearing act before I become the nanny to those brats."

"I know you're not talking about running away again, Imani."

"But I'm tired, Kenya. I've been in foster care since I was seven. Had five mothers already, and I ran from every one of them. I can take care of myself now. Only problem is, they don't give you any help with an apartment when you're just sixteen."

"So why don't you wait?"

"Why should I? Mike is nineteen, got him a little studio."

"Don't do that."

"Then I can work. And look." Imani said, reaching into her pocket. "He bought me a cell phone."

"Does she know you have it?" Kenya asked, looking at the sleek, silver picture phone.

"Are you crazy? She would take it away. I had to fight about my iPod and I bought it myself. That's why I'm telling you, I gotta get out of there!"

"Yeah, but you don't really know this guy."

"Yes I do. I've been seeing Mike for what . . . six weeks now."

"That's not a long time."

"But he's already lookin' out. He met me on Friday and gave me the money to get a manicure and pedicure. And next week he's gonna give me the money to get my hair done."

"That sounds good, but—"

"I'm tellin' you. He's the one."

"Okay, well, then, what's the rush?" Kenya asked.

"Mike is like . . . I'm flippin' over this dude, you don't know!"

Kenya returned Imani's loving smile, appreciating what she was feeling. "Okay, but just don't do anything crazy—yet." Mindful of the time, Kenya looked at her watch. "We gotta go. Oh, give me your cell number."

"I don't have any paper."

"That's alright, I'll write it in my hand. Go ahead, I'm listening . . ."

AWAITNG AN opportunity to speak to Kenya, Leron Tatum leaned against the recessed wall opposite her math class, feigning interest in a textbook. Wearing what he called his Lucky Jersey—gray and black and long-sleeved—with a platinum chain around his neck—he knew she would notice him.

"Hey, hey, hey," Leron called, grabbing Kenya gently by the arm as she swept by. "How you doin'?"

" . . . Alright," she responded, hesitating.

"I saw you in the gym the other day."

As she was drawn into his brown eyes, her memory temporarily failed her, having no recollection of yesterday, today or even an hour ago. ". . . You did?" she managed to ask.

"Yeah, you were wearing these black shorts, a white T-shirt."

"I – I don't remember seeing you," she frowned awkwardly.

"I got gym the same time as you do. I saw you from the other side."

"Oh."

"Cute," he said, pulling her out of the way of traffic.

"Huh?"

"Your voice. It's cute."

His friends, standing nearby and surreptitiously urging him on, pretended to be engaged in small talk.

"So what's your name?"

"Last call!" her teacher announced suddenly, appearing at the door. "Let's go! Door's closing."

"I gotta run," Kenya said, looking back remorsefully. "I'll talk to you later."

Feeling outside herself, she walked into class feeling feather-light. His soft, warm touch still lingered on her skin.

"Kenya Robinson," Mr. Filospian said.

"I'm here."

Captured in the sudden, joyous web of sensation, she slid easily into her assigned seat. She stretched her hands out in front of her, then frowned at her uneven, unpolished nails and thought of getting a manicure. She stared at the formulas on the board, barely able to focus. The room had become hers and hers only. The people turned to objects, their voices into songs and her thoughts ran wild with possibilities. *A boy like that is talking to me? Had the new hairstyle made the difference? The way I coordinated my clothes? Or the way they're fitting? Hmmm . . .*

Leron was waiting outside when the bell rang.

"You know I had to come back. I wasn't finished."

"What were you sayin'?" Kenya asked.

"Wait a minute," he paused, reading a text message on his cell phone. "What was I thinking, I could have texted you."

"I don't have a text . . . I mean a cell phone. We're not supposed to be using them in school anyway, right?"

"Somethin' like that," he replied as they began to walk. "What's your name again?"

"Kenya."

"That's sweet. Fits you."

"It does?" Kenya was blushing.

"Yeah. I'm Leron. I know somebody's got a claim on you. He goes to this school?"

"Claim? No."

Stalled in the congestion of hallway traffic, he slipped a piece of paper into her hand.

"What's the matter?" he asked, observing the look in her face.

"Nnn-nothing."

"Give me a call."

His brown eyes mesmerized her, and her heart felt as though it had descended into her stomach.

"Yeah . . . okay."

Flirtatiously he raised his bushy eyebrows and said, "I'll get wit'chu later."

As Kenya walked to her next class, the afternoon sun shone brighter, the hallways lit up, and everything around her came alive. Being in the mainstream of things surely had its advantages, she thought. Things were already looking up.

five

Thank God for Friday. Dreary, slightly drizzling and all, everyone welcomed its arrival. After school Kenya took the long route and walked down the boulevard, window-shopping. She loved picturing herself in some of the hottest urban gear and scanning the racks for sales. Walking past a side street, she stopped abruptly, taking notice of all the cars that appeared to have a layer of snow on them. Only no snow had fallen that day. Curious, she followed the stares of those around her as a small red Mercedes swept by with a big camera fastened to the window.

"They're shooting a movie," she heard someone say.

Fascinated by the production and seeing a famous star, Daniel Petrees, Kenya watched several different takes of the car scene as it spun around the block.

Late getting home, Kenya cleaned up the kitchen and decided to get a jump on dinner.

"That's you, Mommy?" she asked, startled by the door when it slammed.

"That all depends on how you look at it," a masculine voice responded.

"Chad, I thought you were Mommy."

"Well, I am. An extension of her, anyway." He lifted the lids of the pots, curious about the meal. "Got you cookin' huh?"

"Get out of there!" Kenya insisted, pushing him aside. "You can taste the spaghetti when it's ready."

"Am I gonna live that long?" he asked, moving over to the sink.

"Can't you wash your hands in the bathroom?"

"Why, when I can do it right here?" He held out his wet hands. "This way I have you to personally assist me," he said as Kenya tore off a paper towel and handed it to him. "What man could resist this service?"

"I wouldn't get so comfortable if I were you," Kenya told him. "I won't always be around here."

"And where you goin'?"

Kenya looked at her brother, who turned into Leron right before her eyes. Through her imagination, she jumped into the future, where she and Leron had become Mr. and Mrs. She eyed his movements in a daze.

"What's on your mind?" Chad asked, catching the look. "Somebody of the opposite sex?"

Kenya felt embarrassed. Did her brother have X-ray vision? "What are you talking about?"

"Yeah, huh," he grunted, dismissing his question, but not his thoughts. "I know you're not tryin' to look at none of these boys around here."

"Boys?"

"You heard what I said."

"I heard what you said but—"

"Then keep listening," he said, cutting her off while flipping through the newspaper. "You got betta things to do than gettin' caught up with some do nothin' dude. They only want one thing."

"That's what you want."

"That's none of your business what I want."

"You make it my business when you have three or four girls calling here all the time."

"Those are my friends."

"So . . . then I should be able to have friends, too."

"Don't work like that."

"Why not?"

"Them boys ain't tryin' to be your friend. How many times I gotta tell you."

"How do you know?"

" 'Cause I know . . . so shet up and do what I tell you to do."

Sulking, Kenya turned away. For the first time a boy made her realize that she existed in the world, and her brother poisoned the fantasy. How would she be able to make phone calls or receive them with big brother watching her? How could she experience the pleasure of being somebody's girl, especially someone as cute and popular as Leron?

"Anyway, Mommy said you need to do something with those wires," Kenya said, changing the subject, "before somebody gets hurt."

"I looked at them already. The outlet needs a front plate and some wire nuts."

"Well call the landlord and tell him."

"For the twenty-fifth time? He didn't answer the first call or the fifth call, so what I'm s'pose to do . . . keep calling him?"

"Call somebody else, then," Kenya urged. "Mommy said she thinks Mali got shocked the other day."

Chad got up and pulled out a roll of masking tape from the kitchen drawer, leaving her alone to finish cooking.

AFTER DINNER, feeling wildly energetic, Kenya completed her kitchen chores: she cleared the table, washed and dried the dishes, swept the floor, and the whole time she sang R&B love songs.

Returning to her room to start her homework, she became locked under a spell of illusion while reading. Between every other sentence, Leron's face faded into her view; quick shots of innocent romance dramatized in full color. That warm and fuzzy feeling creeping into her sparked the flame of infatuation, and it was new and exciting.

I should call him now. No. What I am saying, it's been a few days. I'm gonna have to sneak into Mommy's room to use her phone. Then again, if I do that he'd see my number—unless I block it— but if I don't and he calls and Nugget Head finds out, it's gonna be all kinds of drama up in here. I could use the pay phone by Evelyn's Chicken House, but it's too late to get out without having to answer a thousand questions. And who uses pay phones any more, even if you don't have a cell phone. Just tell Leron the truth. No! That's too embarrassing.

She rolled over on her back, gripping her notebook. Her eyes bored into the ceiling that, in her fantasy view, turned into a perfect new sky that crowned the world under which she and Leron lived.

What about Imani's phone? Yeah!

Kenya jumped up, tiptoed down the stairs, went into her mother's room and dialed Imani's number.

"Hello?"

"Imani, it's me, Kenya."

"You just caught me. I was about to turn this phone off."

"Why you turning it off?"

" 'Cause she's on way home."

"Oh yeah, that's right, she doesn't know you have the phone."

"Nope, so whassup."

"I want to use your phone."

"What? You want me to do a three-way?"

"Mmm, nah. I'll just use it when I see you."

"No problem. Wait. I'm not gonna see you again until what . . . Tuesday."

"That's why I'm calling you now. I want to meet you somewhere before then. Whatchu doin' tomorrow?"

"Tomorrow . . . what's tomorrow, Saturday?"

"Uh huh."

"Mmm . . . I've got to watch these brats of hers tomorrow night. Oh, and I got to do laundry. I go to that spot, you know the Laundromat on the boulevard. I have some—"

"That's perfect! I can meet you there."

"What time are you talkin' about? 'Cause I'm gonna be there from like . . . 10:30 till about 12:30 . . . depending on how crowded it is."

"Okay, I should be there around . . . noon?"

"Alright. Who you wanna call, anyway?"

"I was waiting for you to ask. Imani . . . this man . . . okay, he's in the tenth grade— Oh, my God!"

"Whaaaat."

"Remember Casio, the real fine dude that used to come to church with his baby sister, the cute little girl with the pretty eyes?"

"Um . . . that was a long time ago."

"Yeah, 'cause you haven't been to church in like . . . forever."

"I gotta think back because I was staying on Shephard Street then . . . with that old lady."

"Yeah, you remember. Tanisha used to be all up in his face but then later we found out he wasn't into girls."

"Oh . . . I know who you're talkin' about."

"Yeah, well he looks better than that!"

"Uh oh!"

"That's right. I didn't know he had been checking me out. Out of the blue, he came up to me and started talking, gave me his number and asked if I wanted to hang out."

"No he didn't. Not you."

"What do you mean, not me? You tryin' to be funny?"

Imani started laughing. "No, I just can't picture it . . . you, the virtuous one, with a male somebody."

Kenya laughed, too. "Well I couldn't see it either until I met him. He's way taller than me. Not really, if I'm wearing shoes—and *fine!* Got these real dark features and wears one of these thick ponytails. Wait till you meet 'im."

"Why don't you call him from home?"

" 'Cause I'm living with the detective. If Chad finds out, we'll end up fighting. He'll tell my mother and I-I-I-I don't want to deal with all of that."

"Get a life! Whassup with these people and all these restrictions?"

"I don't know."

"Ay, I see her pulling up right now. I gotta go. See you tomorrow."

"Okay, bye."

BY THE time Kenya arrived at the Laundromat in the strip mall, Imani had already dried most of her clothes. It was warm, crowded and lively inside smelling like bleach, softener and hot dogs. They were on sale in the snack bar for a dollar. Imani looked like an Indian with her black-and-white bandana tied around her long, thick mane, which she seldom wore loose.

"Like that Pocahontas look."

"Hey, what took you so long?" she asked, greeting Kenya with a hug.

"Trying to get away from my brothers," Kenya replied, still breathing hard from the brisk walk. "The little ones wanted to come with me, but I told them it would be better for them to stay with my mother 'cause I had some studyin' to do."

Imani's clothes looked bright and white as Kenya watched her folding them. "I need to take some lessons from you. You keep your things so nice and neat."

"Huh," she grunted. "Jumping from foster home to foster home, you learn to take care of your things. You have to, or you might not have any."

"It's not gonna be much longer," Kenya said softly, feeling sorry for her friend.

"Oh, I know it's not," Imani responded, watching the music video. " 'Cause I'm out of there."

"Stop talking like that."

"You think I'm playin' . . . you watch."

"No, I know you're not, that's what scares me. Don't run away like you did the last time, Imani. It took over two years for you to work your way back here."

"Ay, but I gotta cell phone now. We can keep in touch."

"I don't want to hear none of that today. Give me the phone."

KENYA paced the pavement, withstanding the wind and rehearsing her thoughts before finally getting up the nerve to call. With each ring her heart palpitated, nervous in anticipation.

"Hello."

"Hello, Leron."

"Who's this?"

"It's Kenya?"

"Who?"

"Kenya, remember . . . you saw me the other—"

"Oh, whassup? Yeah, what took you so long to call?"

"Umm . . . I-I got busy. Some things I had to do."

"Yeah, 'cause I expected you hear from you that day. Where you at?"

"Right now . . . I'm with my cousin at the supermarket."

"Whose number is this?"

"Um . . . my cousin's cell, but we share it."

There was a brief pause. Kenya could hear other people in the background.

"Yeah, so, whenever I see you at school, you're always by yourself . . . and movin'."

"I'm so busy most of the time."

"What about after school? You got some free time?"

"Yeah. I mean, no. I work on Tuesdays and Thursdays. What about you?"

"What about me?"

"You have a job?"

"Not right now . . . which is probably good. If I did, I wouldn't have any time for you."

"For me?"

"Yeah, why don't you hang out with me for a minute after school?"

Kenya sucked her breath in quietly as she could feel herself heating up on the inside.

"Hello?"

"Yeah, I'm here."

"Can you hear me?"

"Yeah, I can hear you."

"I said, let's get together after school . . . you know, just chill. Know what I'm sayin'?"

"Um . . . I'll have to see 'cause. . . . there's some other things I have to do."

"So whatchu sayin'? You don't have time for me?"

"No, I'm not sayin' that. I just have to make some changes."

"Whatcha doing next Tuesday?"

"Working, remember?"

"Yeah, that's right. What about Wednesday?"

"Mmm . . . maybe."

"Why don't you hit me up later and let me know."

"Okay."

"'Iight. Ay, I can reach you at this number?"

"Yeah."

"'Iight, later."

"Okay, bye."

With lighthearted exuberance, Kenya walked back inside the Laundromat as she reviewed what she had said. Much of it was not true, but in her nervousness her responses simply fell out of her mouth.

"So what did he say?" Imani asked.

"He wants to take me out next week."

Imani held her hand up and together they slapped each other high-fives.

"What are you gonna tell your mother?"

"I don't know, but I'll figure something out."

"You're gonna be sneaking around like me."

"Nah, I'm just thinking. I'll go out with him a couple of times and if I'm feeling him like that, I'll tell my mother."

"Sounds like a plan to me. Oooh, and when I start workin' at the Hip-Hop Sub Shop, y'all can come over there to eat."

"Yeah, that's right!"

Looking out the front window, watching people coming and going about their lives, Kenya was excited, an inner thrill she had never known before.

"The rest of my clothes are finished," Imani said, turning the basket toward the dryer.

"Good. Then we can get out of here. I'll help you fold."

"Cool."

six

Nadira was on special assignment today, attending a youth summit meeting in Manhattan that was scheduled for early afternoon. But before leaving school, she urgently wanted to speak to Kenya. Inside the assistant principal's office, Nadira thumbed vigorously through the student roster to find Kenya's class schedule.

The Special Education corridor was a different world to Nadira, looking at the simplicity of the bulletin boards, the dimensions of the classrooms and the small number of students in them as she walked by. *Okay, her classroom should be right down this hall here. Room 212, 213, 214. No. It's the other way.* When she arrived at Room 203B, it was dark inside. The note on the door read: *"Mr. Friedman is absent today. All math classes will meet in the auditorium."*

Attendance in the auditorium was sizable, as several teachers were absent and substitutes were managing their classes. Raul Sanchez, the school videographer, came in behind her with The League of Nations Club, a multicultural group advocating cultural awareness for all ethnicities attending Telham Park High School.

Sashaying down the center isle to a beautiful rendition of the "Star Spangled Banner" being played at the piano, Nadira scanned the assembly room of familiar faces, looking for Kenya. The words of the "Star Spangled Banner" attached themselves to the melody and rang out in her head and she found herself singing—*"So proudly we hail at the twilight's . . ."*

Nadira walked up the left aisle of the auditorium and worked her way to the back and then across to the right aisle and back down to the front, hoping to spot her. She strode up the middle aisle once more, searching with a sharp eye, when she happened to look toward the stage.

Expecting to see Mr. Wilson, the school's music teacher, Nadira was astounded when she recognized the profile of the individual sitting at the piano.

Nadira stepped on to the stage in staunch disbelief and watched Kenya working magic, the black and ivory keys obeying her commands as if they were natural extensions of her fingers. Without music sheets she repeated the last verse, adding a different effect, more flamboyant and colorful, pulling Nadira into its grace. *"The land of the free . . ."*

"Kenya, you're gonna make me cry!" Nadira quivered as students applauded.

"Why?" she smiled, happy to see her friend.

"You never told me you could play the piano."

"Oh, this is nothing. I do it for fun."

"Who taught you how to play like that?"

"Nobody," she replied mildly, trying to suppress a smile.

"No. No. You don't just do this off the top of your head. Somebody had to teach you something."

"No, for real. I just play what I hear. Nobody ever taught me."

Nadira looked at Kenya with bewilderment, still dumbstruck, yet so proud at the same time.

"Play "Sweet Night Inspiration," a boy named Ellis said.

Showing no self-consciousness whatsoever, Kenya began to play softly.

"So you just walk around here with all of this in you? Kenya, I can see it as clear as day. *You* on a Broadway stage . . . CDs, concerts, Hollywood."

"Git outta here."

"No, I'm serious. This is . . . This is . . . I'm telling you, now is the time. Which reminds me why I came looking for you in the first place! Whew! I don't believe you. Anyway, I'm not coming to gym today, but I need a definite yes from you on the audition. This is the last day to sign up."

"Already?" Kenya asked, continuing to play.

"I've been reminding you every few days. Told you it was gonna creep up on you. C'mon, you have to do this."

"I don't know." She replied reluctantly.

"What are you saying, this is your chance! Look, the audition's no different than what you're doing right here. You're on stage, we'll get you a microphone, and all you have to do is sing. Look out there, Kenya," Nadira said, directing her eyes out into the seated area. "It's your world. Only difference is, it's gonna be some student judges and some teachers. I think three students and three teachers, or three and five or five and three, whatever. Anyway, all you have to do is get up there and sing. Do a song acappella like you did in the locker room. Sit here and play the piano too, if you want."

"No, I wouldn't want to do that."

"You gotta be kiddin' me. Your talent is gold! No platinum! Don't you know that?"

Kenya smiled appreciatively, sprinting up and down the keyboard, playing with no practical strategy, following the rhythm resonating inside her.

"I'm looking at you and I still can't believe you can play the piano like this," Nadira mumbled, nodding incredulously. "You could be the new classical wonder. I can't wait for you to be discovered."

Kenya jabbed at the keys with remarkable ease, experimenting with chords and creating tones of splendid elegance.

With a two-finger whistle Nadira attracted Raul, who was pointing his camera toward the stage. "Mira . . . over here." He was going to be a "cinematographer"—or so he told everyone.

Soon a bright light shone on Kenya. "Ladies and gentleman, we have a superstar on the rise," announced Nadira. "Check out this incredible, enormously talented young lady . . . but wait until you hear her sing."

"What's your name?" Raul asked.

"Kenya," she replied bashfully and continued to play chromatic octaves and glissandos up and down the keyboard.

"Robinson," Nadira added. "Kenya Robinson, remember that name."

Raul slowly circled the piano, taking wide-angle shots of Kenya playing.

"That's right, Raul, she's gonna make history for Telham Park High, you watch. Kenya, I'm taking this as a yes . . . that you're officially auditioning for the Spring Talent Search."

Kenya nodded easily.

"I think she agrees," said Raul, shooting her from another side.

"Mission accomplished," Nadira said happily, and hustled out of the auditorium.

AUNT SOPHIE'S bronchial disorder sent her into a series of coughs, interrupting the silence of their reading in the sunroom. Comforting her, Kenya offered her a drink of water and patted her back several times.

Daylight Savings Time was still a few weeks off, but the days had become noticeably longer. Aunt Sophie's gaze returned to the elegance of the bronze sunset outside. "I can smell the spring," she murmured softly.

"What does it smell like?" Kenya asked just to make conversation. She was growing annoyed with the amount of homework she had received from her English class.

"You get a sudden whiff of fresh cut grass on a sunny day."

"But it's still cold outside."

"Oh, but the greens and flowers are growing beneath the earth."

Kenya tossed her English book to the side, frustrated. "This class is hard, and this teacher just keeps piling all this work on us. Sometimes I can't keep up."

"I thought you would be enjoying your English class."

"At first I was, when we were doing the parts of speech . . . well, reviewing it, anyway. But now we're reading short stories and we're supposed to write small reviews. Then at the same time she has us reading these anthologies . . . asking all these complicated questions. Then she wants us to—"

Aunt Sophie began coughing again, prompting Kenya to get up.

"Sit," Aunt Sophie blurted out, waving her hand to direct Kenya to stay seated. "This is why I tell you about keeping up with your writing journal."

"I try, but I have so much work to do. There's just not enough time."

"You must make the time, anxious one. It's called discipline."

"And then I have to—"

"Take it easy. You have to be open to receive it, or else it won't come."

"Receive what?"

Aunt Sophie coughed a few more times, recovered, and began slowly. "The lessons that lead to discipline. And everybody's lessons come differently. It's not an instant thing, you know."

Kenya scratched her head and folded her arms, feeling discomfited. "Okay, I gotta read, do all these writing exercises, and we have to write this essay. And now you're telling me I gotta learn another lesson on how to get through these lessons."

"See, now, that kind of attitude will constipate you. That's the problem with young people. I was a feisty bird once upon a time too, ya know. Ready to fly at the drop of a dime . . . only it never occurred to me I needed wings."

"What do you mean?" Kenya asked, cocking her head sideways.

Aunt Sophie looked off in silence. Then she came back, fondling the silver key that hung around her neck. "You've got to sharpen your tools . . . if you want to be effective. The rules of grammar mean nothing if they're not applied. And to amply apply them, you have to declog your system."

Kenya wasn't very familiar with the word "declog," but understood its meaning in this context. Sometimes she couldn't keep up with Aunt Sophie's theories and philosophies. Remaining quiet for a moment, her thoughts began drifting as she aimlessly flipped through the pages of her textbook. Leron was on her mind, and it was evident to the wise old woman that she was distracted.

"On that essay thing there, what's your topic?" Aunt Sophie asked, dismissing Kenya's unproductive thoughts.

"I'm not sure yet."

Aunt Sophie coughed a few more times, muffling them with her handkerchief.

"It's supposed to be a creative writing assignment, so she told us to think out of the box. You know, think of a topic that might make interesting reading, but something we might like. Okay, I don't mean like . . . if you like shopping, playing music or sports. She said to write about something that we find motivating or life-enhancing."

"You mean like something that propels you forward, inspires you?" Aunt Sophie clarified.

"Yeah, like that."

"Oh, now you could be talking about fishing . . . could be writing, could be picking cherry tomatoes. Anything that allows you to be free in your thinking, or something that pushes your button. You like to sing, don't you?"

"Sure do."

"You dream about it?"

"Not in my sleep so much. But at night sometimes, I imagine all these things while I'm singing."

"Like what?"

"Different things. Like I see me traveling all over the world and I have all this money and— You know, like I picture it and then it's like a movie I'm watching."

"Well, there you go. Tell us about the process. How the act of dreaming motivates you to do better and reach your goals. You said you like to do this dreaming at night, right?"

"Yes."

"Then start from there."

Clueless, Kenya crossed her legs and gazed off into nowhere. "But I don't know how to set it up. I can write something if you tell me what to write about, but right off the top of my head is—"

"The best way to start designing your essay, really, is by no design at all. That's called open-ended writing."

"Huh?"

"You start by pouring out your thoughts. You know, what happens to you when you start dreaming? How do you feel? Where do you go in the dreams? Put it down on paper. It'll all come together later."

"Just write down whatever I'm thinking?"

"If it comes to your mind, write it down. In my day, child, you weren't living if you didn't have dreams. And I'd write them all down. They were like the road map leading to any destiny you wanted to reach. 'Specially during the time when I was dancing in the clubs."

"Not you, Aunt Sophie. Dancing?"

"Who, me?" Aunt Sophie delicately put her hand to her throat, acting coy. "Shoot…could cut a rug with the best of 'em. I was a good dancer, too. Got hired in all the swinging clubs then. Maynard's. BK's Den—"

"What kind of dancing were you doing?" Kenya interrupted, breaking her train of thought.

"Any kind. Line dancing . . . Oh, but the craze then was the Swing. We would Swing 'til we were delirious. Sometimes 'til the sun came up."

"Really?"

"I was living in Harlem then. Just graduated from Springhard College for Girls. Lemme see uh . . . now that would be May of uh . . . 1939. Yes, ma'am. That next month, June, I was on the bus headed to New York, New York. Now, according to my mother, I was supposed to be coming up here to find a teaching job. Well." Aunt Sophie briefly paused, and a sly little grin passed over her face. "That was what I told *her* I was aiming to do 'cause there were no good teaching jobs down there for coloreds."

Kenya sneered. "I hate that word coloreds. Sounds like—"

"We didn't like it, either . . . eventually changed it, too. Then we moved on because we had bigger fish to fry. Anyway, I was living in a room on 137th Street. Room wasn't big enough for me to change my mind in, and I working at Club Castaway. Now that was a partying palace! Big bands and all kind of dancin' and singin' goin' on. Some of everybody famous came through there. That's when I fell in love with this musician. He was just visiting. See, back in that time, different musicians played gigs from town to town, whenever or however they could get work, ya know. Child, I got to stuttering when I first laid eyes on him." A big smile drew up on Aunt Sophie's face as she looked back out into the fleeting sunset.

"We fell in love right then and there," she continued, "and after about two weeks, he wanted to take me on the road with him—I'll never forget it. Philadelphia was his next stop. And lemme tell you . . . the way I felt about that man, I was willin' ta go. The end of the earth wouldn't have been too far to go with him, huh."

Aunt Sophie's laughter of her memories filled the room, and Kenya enjoyed watching her animated gestures as she wandered back in time. Caught up in the intrigue of the story, she had forgotten about her own concerns.

"So, what happened?"

She grunted and chuckled and soon came back to the point. "Ahhh . . . he knew he couldn't afford a bus ticket for me, and he wasn't allowed to bring any guests with him. It was tight as it was on that crowded bus. But we just couldn't see parting. Now we were desperate for each other and all, but he couldn't afford to give up his gig, not even for me. See 'cause I could get a job anywhere. I tell you . . . when I think about it . . . the foolish things you do when you're young," Aunt Sophie shook her head, smiling softly.

"So what did y'all do?"

"He smuggled me right on that bus with him. Slipped me in the bass fiddle cover and laid me down in the back."

"No he didn't!"

"Yes I did! I was chasing my dreams then. Anything I wanted to do. Huh, and was happy to do it. Shoot, the whole ride down, he slipped me snacks and cheese sandwiches and massaged me to keep me from getting stiff. I wrote about that adventure for days. I called it "The Sweetest Ride Known to Cheese.""

They laughed out loud together.

"Aunt Sophie, you for real?"

"Don't I look real? 'Course I am."

Kenya turned away, cutting her eyes with skepticism. She was well aware that Aunt Sophie had avoided her question.

"Now get to writing," she ordered. "If you got dreams, you got a whole lot to write about."

Aunt Sophie's story prompted Kenya to begin jotting down her thoughts. Reflecting on her late night dreams, she wrote phrases and incomplete sentences, none of which appealed to her. She wanted to write an essay as captivating and exciting as Aunt Sophie's story. Looking toward the horizon, she drifted into a private dream . . . .

Leron stepped through the French glass doors into the foyer of a house set in a Southern countryside chalet. Wearing a white linen suit and walking with a proud gait, he strode toward her against a backdrop of verdant mountains. The crystal day with its benevolent sun coached the fertile earth to a rich, velvety green.

"What took you so long? I've been looking for you," he said, his eyes searching pleasantly over her face. "You're just like I imagined you."

Kenya wasn't clumsy or careless; she was as even as the breeze that whisked by her upturned face. He kissed her sweetly on the nape of her neck and caressed the softness of her cheek. He looked at her with smiling eyes while his strong arms encircled the small of her back. Enveloped in the strong protectiveness of his powerful arms, the desire to belong to him completely seemed to move the earth beneath her.

Finally . . . inspiration came. Over and over, Kenya read the first three lines. Then she checked them again for spelling and grammar. By now, Aunt Sophie was starting to doze off into one of her quick naps, and Kenya decided to take a shot at it one final time before moving on to her other work.

"What did you come up with?" Aunt Sophie said, waking up suddenly.

"Nothing, really. I wrote some things down. I mean . . . because the essay is not due for weeks. But it's gonna be twenty-five percent of our mid-term grade. So that's what all these exercises are supposed to be leading to."

"Well, then . . . see," she yawned. "This is good, but don't wait until the last minute and get yourself all worked up. Never too early to start putting it together. Structure up your rough draft. Then keep working on it, little by little. Every day you live is gonna bring something different to it. You'll see." Aunt Sophie peered over at Kenya's page. "Let me see me what you've got."

Reluctantly, Kenya handed it over to her. The first few lines read:

> Alone in my windowless room, night comes. When the house gets quiet I sit up in my bed completely masked by my covers. My fingers creep along the sides of my blanket that have become the walls to my secret cave.

"It's a start," Aunt Sophie praised. "What you have to —"

"Can I see you for a second?" Imani said, interrupting them.

"Give me a minute, Aunt Sophie. I'll be right back," Kenya said and exited the sunroom. "Whassup?"

"You got a message."

"I do?"

"Yep. He said he wants you to call him."

"Oh!" Kenya was excited.

"We're out of here in the next forty-five minutes anyway, and I'm going to stop by the Hip-Hop Sub Shop before I go back into lockdown."

"You mean home."

"Pssss, whatever. Here, hurry up and make this call 'cause I have to get back to the recreation room."

Kenya moved out into the hallway and called Leron's number.

"Hello, Leron. It's Kenya. How you doin'?"

"I'm good. What's goin' on wit'chu?"

"Nothing, um . . . I got your message."

"We hookin' up tomorrow?"

"Uh . . . I'm not sure."

"I figured we could go hang out at my uncle's crib, watch some videos or somethin'."

"Your uncle's?"

"Yeah. He's hardly ever there, and we could have some privacy."

Kenya wasn't comfortable with his suggestion. "Um . . . maybe we could get something at McCuller's or—"

"I'm not really into crowds. Especially when I'm with my girl, know what I'm sayin'."

"Yeah."

"And it's not far. He lives right there on Belrose. You gonna come?"

"I'm not sure, I'll try."

"You're not scared or nothin'. I mean it's not like I'm gonna take advantage of you."

"I know," Kenya responded, shrugging prettily.

"Well, call me later and let me know."

"Um . . . I think I'm gonna try to make it. Can you meet me on the third floor? My last class is—"

"Nah . . . um, I get out before you do and I have a couple of stops to make."

"Okay."

"Why don't we hook up down there by the gas station? You know, where the bread factory is . . . on the corner of Edgemont."

"I know where it is."

"Meet me at like . . . 2:45."

"I'll see you in school tomorrow. Let's talk about it then. What time do you have lunch?"

"Uh, sixth or seventh, I forget."

"I got lunch fifth period.

"That's not gonna work."

"Well . . ."

"Look, if I don't see you in school, just meet me on Edgemont."

"Okay."

"Iight, peace."

"Bye."

On her way home, Kenya thought of ten different stories she could tell her mother that would open up the opportunity for her to spend the afternoon with Leron. Then, suddenly, in a light-bulb moment, it came to her. *The Telham Park Idol Search!* She knew her mother would be thrilled to know she was auditioning and her brother would have no objections.

KENYA LIKED her bathwater toasty warm. The stress of the day melted away as she sank into the tub and noticed the water level rose. She followed the rainbow in the big bubble set high above the shimmery blanket of suds underneath the glow of scented candles she'd purchased from the ninety-nine cents store. Between the maze of multicolored streams she envisioned a crystal palace set on a lush green estate with white horses outside and a Baby Grand piano set in a lavish conservatory. She could almost feel the cool grass underfoot; the image appeared so vividly in her mind. Her fingers keyed the music to "I Believe In Love," and she hummed the tune softly with her eyes closed.

Kenya dried herself completely before coming out of the bathroom, which had held her happily hostage for more than an hour. Upon entering her room, she fell back on her bed, too excited to think about anything except Leron and tomorrow. *"What am I going to wear?"* she asked herself time and again as she clipped her nails. Jumping to her feet, she looked in the mirror. The two braids were cute. *Hmm, looked better the other way I think. Leron seemed to like it. I want another kind of look, though.* She grabbed the rubber band, unraveling her thick hair. She let out a frustrated sigh and turned sideways to view her profile. Then she smiled admiring her petite, curvaceous figure.

"Kenya!" her mother called, shattering the moment.

"Yes."

"What are you doing?"

Kenya pulled her hair up forward, and then pushed it back again, forgetting to answer her mother. *Maybe I could cut my long sides. Bangs would be cute. No. My hair is too curly. Kinky curls look good. All I have to do is wash it.*

She couldn't remember the last time she'd been to the hair salon. Thinking back, she realized it the day before she graduated from middle school. In fact, there was the proof, sitting right there in front of her—the five-by-seven picture of her in an antique silver frame. Kenya gazed at the photo and saw a very shy, overprotected, underdeveloped outcast.

"Kenya!" her mother called out again. "You finished your homework? *Indigo Village* is on."

"Not yet," was Kenya's reply as she opened her sea-shelled box and took out her brush. She reached for the Indian hemp in the top dresser drawer and dug deep around its edges, slapped the herbal pomade into the center of her hands, and carefully slid it all over her hair. An instant sheen woke up the dullness, highlighting a subtle body of waves. She ran down to the bathroom and wet her brush and stroked her hair until there wasn't a single strand out of place—just a row of waves, smooth and silky. She grabbed a scarf and tied up her head, looking forward to seeing its outcome.

seven

Kenya arose early on Wednesday morning, feeling anxious. A different kind of confidence came with her clean, modern look and neatly manicured nails. After some excessive primping, she slid into her fitted jeans and a new sweater.

"Mornin' Yonkies," she greeted, kissing Mali and Morocco, who were seated at the table.

"You smell good," said Mali, giving her one of his sticky kisses.

"Don't I always smell good?"

"You look good, baby," her mother noted, spooning out oatmeal on a plate. "How long's the audition rehearsal gonna be today?"

"All afternoon," Kenya replied, reaching for the newspaper. Before reading the headlines, her eyes fell to the bottom of the page to the index:

Horoscope...page 38.

> **Virgo:** Today, your essence is attractive to others. Be daring and not afraid to show

love to the one who loves you. Caution: Be a vigilant observer of those who make claims of love as opposed to flimsy romantic encounters. The things you desire in a relationship are simple: honesty, generosity, adventure and hearty laughter.

"What time are you coming home?" Kenya's mother asked. "Kenya."

"Huh?"

"What time do you think you'll be getting home?"

"Probably around . . . five-thirty, six."

"You got enough money?"

"Uh huh."

"Okay, but I need you to call me if you're going to be any later."

"I think you need to watch her," said Chad, entering the kitchen. He came up from behind her and squeezed the back of her neck.

"Git outta here!" Kenya snapped, closing the newspaper.

He reached for it and took his seat at the table. "Think you slick," he mumbled. "I already told you. Let me find out . . ."

Wanting to escape Chad's obvious suspicions, she downed a cup of tea and half of a bran muffin, delivered her morning parting ritual—hugs and 'Love You's'—quickly pecked her mother on the cheek, and shot out of the door.

KENYA SNATCHED away the spider web netting her forehead while moving cautiously down the uneven stairs in Leron's uncle's basement. She suddenly had reservations about being there and paused, glancing over the open space.

"Go ahead," Leron directed, nudging her forward from behind.

He flicked the switch of an old crooked floor lamp and lit up the space. It was eerie décor of mismatched furniture, peeling walls, and dusty surfaces. "It could use a little work," Leron admitted, looking around curiously.

Kenya stepped easily around the green velvety sofa, looking at old pictures and odd objects, hoping to get warm. The thick stack of vinyl record albums piled up on a wooden chest intrigued her.

"You alright?" he asked.

"It's kinda chilly," she replied, observing the cover of an old group that her mother was a fan of.

Leron's eyes darted over the room and into the kitchen area. He found a small electric heater and plugged it into a nearby outlet. An old portable radio, the size of a shoebox, sat on top of the kitchen counter. A wire hanger bent into the shape of a triangle served as its antenna. When he turned the radio on, a bolt of static startled her, but it soon slid into clear, definite sound. He searched the dial and found a contemporary jazz station, then disappeared into the bathroom.

Sitting down, she sank low into the cushion of the dated sofa. Transporting her thoughts to the scales and melodies of the piano composition was an attempt to soothe her inner angst.

"Take off your coat," Leron said, joining her. "Yeah, you need to get comfortable," he mumbled, promptly assisting her. He tossed her coat to the other end of the couch and slid over close to her.

"This is a privilege right here . . . sittin' next to the new idol."

"Idol?"

"I heard you were auditioning for the Spring Idol Search."

"Where'd you hear that?"

"Doesn't matter. So this means my girl can sing, huh."

Kenya giggled softly and looked away.

"So why don't you sing somethin' for me. I know the AM radio joint is kinda busted, but you can make your own music, c'mon."

"No . . . I can't just sing like that."

"You're gonna be singing in front of an audience, so what do you mean you can't sing like that."

"Not for one person."

"Oh, I'm just a person to you?"

"No," Kenya laughed sweetly. "It's just hard for me to start singing on the spot like that."

"It's just hard for me," he mimicked, stretching to reach her unusually high pitch.

Kenya was laughing.

"Look, pretend like I'm gonna be your toughest critic. Go ahead, sing for me."

"Nnn-no."

"I don't get it. You're gonna get up there in front of five hundred people, but you can't sing for one of me."

"It's hard to explain. I don't know . . . it just feels like a job when it's a lot of people. You just go out there and do it."

"Okay then, if you're too shy to sing for one person . . . then sing with me, c'mon." Leron searched his memory for something popular and began bobbing his head and snapping his finger. "Um . . . what's the words . . .

> *"My days have been long without you*
> *The visions I've dreamed seem doubtful"*

"C'mon, you know the song. Help me out."

> *"My days have been long without you*
> *The visions I've dreamed seem doubtful"*

And then he leaped into the chorus:

> *"You're living inside my head*
> *And living inside my heart"*

His notes were hard and flat, but there wasn't an ounce of embarrassment in him. It was hilarious to Kenya.

"Oh, so you're laughing at me. Cool. I can handle that."

Kenya was warmed by his friendly way; his cool and unpretentious spontaneity.

Settling the mood, he took another leap. "Okay, now I'm being for real. I'm glad you're here."

"Why?"

"So we could hang out. I can look at you . . . and get close. You know you got some pretty eyes." Gingerly, he massaged her shoulder, and the spicy blend of his masculine cologne cut through the stale, musty smell of the basement. "What about you? Why are you here? Tell me the truth."

His hand gently stroked the back of her neck. Kenya could feel her insides trembling as she searched for the right words to say. "I wanted . . . I thought we'd get to know each other."

"Das whassup."

Kenya focused her gaze straight ahead of her and continued a nervous fidget with her fingers that was barely controllable.

"How come you so shy?" he whispered, sliding his hand down her back.

The foreign touch of a young man's hand sent a stream of electricity down her spine, causing her to twitch reflexively. "I don't know, just . . . I was always shy."

"Can't be shy with me, come here," he said, turning her face toward his. His irresistible, brown-eyed gaze weakened her. And then he closed the distance between them.

Kenya dodged his aim, turning her face toward the kitchen, noticeably uncomfortable now.

"You're not still cold, are you?"

"No."

"Look at me. You're not scared?" he asked, pressing his gaze on her.

Kenya nodded a "no" and looked away.

"You sure?"

"Not scared . . . a little uncomfortable, maybe."

He raised his eyebrow, feigning disbelief and pressed his hand on his chest. "With me?"

"Well . . ."

Rethinking his strategy, he moved away Kenya and walked over to the table. "We'll have to get you to relax."

"You have any brothers and sisters?" Kenya asked, attempting to switch the subject and change the mood.

"Two sisters," he replied dryly. He didn't pretend to have the slightest interest in her question. Into his pocket he went and pulled out a small stack of single dollar bills. "Want some Chinese food? An order of chicken wings or somethin'?"

"No. I'm good."

"You sure?"

"Umm huh."

His eyes passed over her, only this time they were cold and inattentive. He went into the refrigerator, popped open a can of grape soda and gulped down a good portion of it. He eyed her critically from the distance. "Want some?" he asked.

"No, I'm okay." Kenya buried her cold hands underneath her thighs to warm them.

When he returned, he plopped down on the sofa and checked his cell phone for messages. He attempted to make a phone call but changed his mind.

"So, what do you want to do?"

"What do you mean?" Kenya asked.

"I brought you here thinkin' you know—like we got a real connection, dig me—but you just brush me off."

"I'm not brushing you off, I'm just sayin'—" Kenya paused and began fidgeting as her words got caught up in her throat.

He showed no sympathy or concern as his eyes bored into hers. "Come here," he said. Inch by inch, he closed the gap between them, aiming at her mouth. His slippery tongue on her lips triggered another spinal twitch, causing her to back away. Aggressively, he leaned into her until she was pinned against the sofa. Under the pressure, she tussled and turned her face away from him.

"Why you gettin' so serious?" she asked.

"I'm a man, what do you expect? You're a woman, right?"

"Yeah."

"You don't act like it."

"Why you say that?"

He backed away, sighing heavily. " 'Cause a woman knows how to read her man and hold his interest."

Kenya was tense. She could feel herself tightening up, unable to maturely respond to his advances.

Abruptly he turned toward her and said, "C'mon, I'm here with you . . . being honest . . . letting you know how I feel and you're . . . just kinda cold."

"I'm not cold. I'm just not . . . like I never—"

"All I'm trying to do is get close to you. I mean . . . if you're gonna be with me, I thought you'd want to share everything with me."

She shot a questioning glance at him and lowered her eyes. Her mind rushed back to all the things she'd heard and been told and tried to apply it to the present, but she felt torn. On the one hand she felt ecstatic that a young man like Leron would want to have her as his girl. Yet her deeper instincts reminded her of her inexperience and the dangers of moving too fast with a young man.

He placed his hand on her thigh and moved it in slow, even strokes. Relax. I'm not gonna hurt you."

"I know, but—"

Before she could utter another sound, his lips were firmly pressed against hers. Kenya could no longer hear the music; it simply faded in the distance.

She swallowed softly and felt the warmth of his heavy breathing and pulled away again.

"Still feel cold?"

"A little bit."

He reached behind the couch and grabbed a blanket and spread it over the two of them. "Better?"

"Um huh."

An encore of the kiss called them both, and this time she responded to his tongue with hers, carefully operating the kiss just as Imani had once explained to her. But then suddenly, his fingers crawled up from her waist onto her breast; creepy as a spider, and in a strong, fast reflex, she gripped his wrist and lowered his hand.

"What's the matter?" he asked arrogantly. "I can't touch you?"

" . . . No, not like . . ."

A soft gasp came out of her as he made another attempt, this time touching the tip of her breast. She pushed his hand away. He tried again and again. Finally, Kenya held onto his wrist and swayed his body away from hers.

"Whatchu doin'?" he asked, growing impatient with her refusals.

"Nothing." To distract his powerful gaze, Kenya pulled away from him and looked at her watch.

"You in a hurry?"

"Um . . . not really . . . yeah, I kinda am. I'm supposed to meet my brother."

Miffed, Leron backed away and said little else to her as she gathered up her belongings and bundled up.

"Am I gonna see you tomorrow?" she asked.

"I don't know, maybe," he shrugged, becoming a stranger, who was cold as ice.

Kenya crept up the stairs and out of the house with a host of conflicting thoughts whirling sickeningly in her head. There were no loving goodbyes, no hugs, no kisses, no escorting her home. No nothing.

AUNT SOPHIE preferred to read in the quiet of her room upstairs instead of the sunroom on Thursday afternoon. Stepping gingerly, Kenya served her a hot cup of green tea with two freshly baked, sugar-free oatmeal cookies she'd purchased on the way in.

"Mmmm, that's a nice presentation you got there," said Aunt Sophie. "Did you make a cup for yourself?"

"No. Not in the mood for tea today."

"Sure got a knack for making things look enticing," commended Aunt Sophie. "Look at the way you sliced that lemon, every piece equivalent in size . . . how you spread the cookies out at an angle . . . and the napkin. You folded it so nice and even. If I didn't know any better, I'da thought I was being served in a restaurant."

Kenya chuckled softly, offering up a half-smile.

"It's what I tell you about your school work," she mumbled. "The way you present it is important."

"Yeah," Kenya agreed dryly, "but you gotta put so much work in it."

"That's right, but even if your work is not perfect, but it's laid out nice and orderly, it'll at least get you some credit. Same thing here. See the tea, these cookies, they could taste like vinegar and cardboard for all the people know, but folks will at least want to reach for it. They may refuse the next bite or the next sip, but you sure did get them excited. See, then, they may want to offer you suggestions on how to make it taste better. Huh, and you'd be surprised. Always somebody in the bunch who gonna say mmmm . . . this is interesting, understand?"

Kenya nodded, a thankful smile on her lips, appreciating the goodness in the elderly woman to help distract her out of her obvious heavy-heartedness. Kenya was preoccupied, still struggling to understand the exchange that had taken place with Leron, and she couldn't bring herself to talk about it to anyone—not even him. He hadn't made any attempts to find her in school, and he hadn't called her, either.

"How you comin' along with your work?"

Kenya's eyes wandered back over to Aunt Sophie, bringing the cup up to her mouth. "Be careful with that tea. It's hot."

She took one teeny sip, and put it down. "Mmm, that's good. Now where are you?"

"Huh?"

"With that essay. You been working on it?"

"Not really."

"Why not?"

"Got a lot on my mind."

"Ya too young for the blues, child. If you get to feeling bad now, tomorrow's gonna look even worse."

"Well, I mean, I've been trying, but it's not coming to me. Why do we have to do all this work anyway?"

"Oh, you wanna complain now. I thought you were happy to move up in the higher classes."

"I-I am, but it's so much work."

"How far you expect to go without working hard?"

"I don't know," Kenya shrugged lamely and looked up and caught Aunt Sophie's penetrating gaze.

"Huh . . . you don't even know what hard work is," she muttered, biting into a cookie. She took her time chewing it and washed it down with three quick sips of tea, never taking her eyes off Kenya. "Hard work was all we knew . . . which is why you don't. Talkin' about hard work, child . . . you have no idea."

A pang of guilt struck Kenya, the tortuous past of her people reflecting through the proud eyes of the elderly woman. Yet even after all Kenya knew she had been through in her life, Aunt Sophie's will was still as strong as steel. "I know ya'll worked hard back then, but—"

"No ya don't," she retorted cuttingly, and folded her small wrinkled hands in front of her as a glimpse of the past revisited her. "I remember the day when Mr. Charlie asked my mother . . . he asked my mother if one of us could pick him some cotton . . . 'bout, 'bout a hundred pounds a week he said, in exchange for some hot cakes and canned sausages from his store. Boyyyy, me and my brothers got to gettin' excited," Aunt Sophie reminisced, smiling tentatively. "Anticipating the goodies, we were anxious to show him how hard we could work. We picked that cotton morning, noon, right up until the sun went down; I mean we worked and worked, happy as pigs in slop—as my grandmother used to say. And Mr. Charlie was well pleased. So pleased he began to challenge us some more . . . and we obliged. We figured the more cotton we picked, the better we could eat . . . and boy, we was eatin' good . . . so we thought. Soon, we were doing about sixty pounds of cotton a day, then eighty, then a hundred, then three hundred."

"Three hundred pounds? How did you lift all that cotton?"

"What you talkin' about, girl? We were like machines, strong as mules. All we ever knew was back-breaking work." Aunt Sophie paused and transferred her gaze up into the sky. "Then it started becoming hard work and I couldn't understand . . . I couldn't understand why Mr. Charlie and his people had such fine things and never worked, and we were out there doing all the hard work, baking in that hot sun and never had nothing. Then my parents sat me down and explained to me how things were . . . but I never accepted it. I tell ya one thing: I set my sights on my education from then on. So when you wanna whine and complain and talk about how hard things are . . . think about all that cotton I picked for you. Broke my back up and everything else . . ."

"Why you tryin' to make me feel guilty, Aunt Sophie?" Kenya asked tremulously, in a low, solemn voice.

"I'm not trying to make you feel any kind of way, but if you are—good! Sometimes it takes a little guilt to wake the people up and get 'em moving. It's not about what you want all the time."

"How about sometimes, Aunt Sophie? Can't I have what I want sometimes?"

"Sure, if it's purposed for you. And it's not for you to expect it either. There's a source far greater than you and His thoughts are not our thoughts."

Kenya sighed heavily, filling up her cheeks with air, feeling a little frustrated with Aunt Sophie's philosophical coaching.

Aunt Sophie took another bite of the last cookie, enjoying it immensely. "And all those things you think you want, you'd be surprised. Where you are now, you don't even know what you want. I know you think you do . . . but listen to the old girl. You don't have a clue." She took another sip of tea, whirling its last bit of content around before she continued. "I remember I was seeing this gentlemen way back in the day when I was pretty and pixie. He was a lot older than I was and would give me the stars on a platter if I asked for it. Unlike my former friend—where we were both young, wildly happy and crazy in love—he was reserved, organized . . . knew how to treat a woman nice."

"How much older was he?"

"I don't really remember," she replied, arching her left eyebrow as her thoughts took her back in time, "but I know he was a good many years ahead of me . . . maybe ten or fifteen. Anyway, he always wanted me close to him, wouldn't let me out of his sight. I thought he was a man helplessly in love. It's what we women think we want, ya know. But honey, all that lovin' ya comes with a price, 'specially with somebody old enough to be ya daddy. Things were good for a hot minute . . . seemed like that anyway. Then I began to feel the strain, ya know, a little uncomfortable at first . . . then every now and again he'd smother me. By the end of that relationship, honey, I was completely suffocated—and sacrificed that time in my life in the process, messing around with that old man. Yes," she smiled indulgently. "It's what we women think we want. Stay with ya own age group . . . with a fella that loves you. Anyway, I vowed then . . . be anxious for nothing. Bible says when you rush things . . . you set yourself back that much further."

Something happened to Kenya while listening to the story and it somehow snapped her out of her haze and whipped her mind to attention. "I'm feeling what you're sayin'," Aunt Sophie. "I just wish I could write essays the way you tell stories."

"No reason you can't."

"Huh . . . my writing doesn't sound interesting to me, so I know it doesn't do anything for anybody else."

"Well, you gotta *make* it interesting."

"But where do you get it from?"

"It's all around you . . . in the rainbow of living. It's what you breathe, what you taste."

"But look, Aunt Sophie." Kenya opened her notebook and tore out the newest installment of her essay. "I call myself trying to get creative, right. I wrote a few more lines, and it took me forever to do that, and then it just sounds like . . . blah."

Aunt Sophie put her glasses on and began reading:

Alone in my windowless room night comes. When the house goes quiet I sit up in my bed completely masked by the covers. My fingers creep along the sides of my blanket that have become the walls to my secret cave. It's pitch black when I open my eyes and I try to see my hands in front of me, but I can't. Through the darkness I drift into this dream world. Then, colors burst alive and I start singing.

"Not bad—you're getting there. Spelling's good. Couple of grammatical boo-boo's here and there—I can correct those—but I can see you're trying to go somewhere with it." Aunt Sophie looked off in silence and slowly began rocking in her easy chair, caressing the silver key around her neck. Then, suddenly, she stopped and removed her glasses. "See, here's what you need to do. You gotta . . . you gotta go to the place when you're writing. You've got to visit the moment. If you're describing a girl . . . a carnival . . . something you like to eat, you've got to look for words that evoke images in your mind . . . sensations in your body . . . sometimes even tickling your taste buds, you know what I mean?"

Kenya pulled at her earlobe, frowning questioningly. "Hmmm . . . when you say 'evoke,' that means to bring out, right?"

"That's right, good, and it shouldn't take you forever to do it, either. Going on and on and on like that . . . you bore the reader. You gotta be stingy with your words . . . but they've got to be the right words."

"But how do you learn how to do—"

"I can't tell you any particular way to do it. No cookie-cutter instructions in writing. You've got to find it within. Well, now, no. I take that back, some things you can learn by reading. You start to expand your vocabulary, play with words and find the ones that evoke a lot of meaning. Like the things I used to write always came to me because I lived it. But even if you haven't actually experienced a thing, you've got to go there in your mind. Hear me?"

"Yes."

"Listen to this, listen. No. Close your eyes first. Keep 'em closed, now, until I finish, okay?"

"Okay."

" 'The big revival they call the Harlem Renaissance was a swingin' time back in the '30s. We'd walk down the busy streets in the sizzling summer heat inhaling the blended aroma of fried chicken, barbecued ribs, whiting fish and collard greens sifting onto the sidewalks. And the soul-drowning blues set your heart a-blazin' as you were tickled by the balmy breeze cooling the nights. We laughed and loved one another under gleaming stars and mild scented wind . . . replacing our fears with poetry. Living and breathing the future was all we knew and there would be no stopping us.' Now open your eyes. . . . Still feeling the feathery ease of that summer breeze?"

"Umm huh."

"Can't you just taste the smoked turkey necks in the greens?"

"I sure can," Kenya chuckled, amazed. "That's sa-lick, Aunt Sophie. You should have been a writer."

"Oooh child, I don't know about that. That requires another set of skills altogether . . . but I can express myself when it's necessary."

"Yeah, but what if you never tasted collard greens and turkey necks? You can't identify the flavor."

"Maybe not, but it'll wake up your taste buds and get your mouth ta salivatin', and that's the whole point."

"Oh, I'm feeling you, girl," Kenya said, laughing. She'd already started thinking, recording in her mind what she had just learned. "Where'd you get that story from, Aunt Sophie?"

"I don't know," she replied, staring off into the wall as if something had suddenly called her attention to it. Then, grabbing hold of the key around her neck, she said, "Probably something I wrote long time ago."

"How do I know you really wrote that?" Kenya needled. "Those could be somebody else's words."

"Doesn't matter. You got the point, didn't you?"

"Sure did."

"Well, good. Now help the old lady up out of this chair and roll me downstairs 'cause I'm gettin' hungry."

eight

"What up, fam?" Christopher greeted everyone, joining Nadira and her friends for lunch at fifth period. Harold was with him.

"Lightning, what's poppin'?" Nadira replied lovingly, giving him a big hug. That had been Christopher's nickname since he was a child, given to him because of his incomparable speed. She looked over at Harold and said, "Hey."

"Look at her, all bright and peppy when she sees you, Chris," Harold observed, "but all I get is 'Hey.' "

"Nothing personal, we just happened to be talkin' about Christopher," Nadira chuckled, tossing a glance between Bianca and Shashawna.

"Yeah, then let me in on it."

"Really and truly, we were talking about Deshon," Bianca corrected Nadira, "but we mentioned *you* first because we know you're the only one who's in touch with him."

"Sure that's all y'all were sayin'?" Christopher asked, biting into a chili dog.

"C'mon now, we're not really gonna let you in on our secrets," Nadira joked, slyly glancing over at her friends. "But seriously, we were talking about Deshon—"

"But then Shashawna told us to taste her homemade lemonade," Bianca continued.

"Oh, you gotta try it," Nadira said. "First thing I thought about was putting a label on it and sellin' it in the stores."

"Bring it on, then," urged Harold, watching her pour a sample into two small plastic cups. He had already sunk his teeth into a tuna sub.

Christopher took a sip, darting his eyes curiously toward all the girls as he swallowed. "Oh, this is good," he commended. "Where'd you learn how to make lemonade like this?"

Staring awkwardly at the pink-colored liquid, Harold said, "Yo, this is serious."

Christopher took another sip, savoring the sharp, tart taste. "I think you put a little ginger in here."

"Forget it," Bianca said. "She won't give up the recipe."

"She doesn't have to. I was just testing my taste buds. But if you're thinkin' about bottling it, you have to disclose the ingredients anyway."

Sandwiching her fat cheeks between her hands, Shashawna said, "There's . . . a-little-bitty-smidgen of ginger spice in it."

"And listen to this," Nadira began explaining, "since there's all-natural ingredients in there, we can get you to be the spokesperson, as if it's an energizer. Make everybody think they can run as fast as you do if they drink it, feel me? We'll get a picture of you in your tracking gear drinking it with that big trophy you just won sitting next to you."

"That's not a bad idea," Harold chuckled. "I'm feelin' that."

"Well, don't be stingy with it now, let me have another cup," Christopher said.

"See, that's how it starts," Nadira rambled on. "We can start selling it right here in the lunchroom."

"Yep, sell it underground," Bianca interjected. She was getting charged.

"I'll give you a dollar right now for a full glass," said Christopher, who had already gulped down the second sample.

"I'll take a full glass, too," said Harold, his mouth full of food.

"Cha-ching-cha-ching, now that's whassup!" Nadira piped. "Do that twenty, maybe thirty times a day, and that's some serious profit, especially being that it doesn't cost that much to make."

"Listen to the entrepreneur over here," remarked Christopher. "But you on the right track, though. Deshon was telling me how profitable the horticulture business is, cuz they got him out in the woods somewhere, doing all kinds of manual labor."

"No, you lyin'!" said Shashawna, bug-eyed.

"Nah, I got his letter right here," Christopher said and pulled out the message. Nadira picked it up and began reading it aloud.

We have to get up at 4:30am I was like a zombie walking around at first, but I got used to it. Have you ever seen a sunrise before? It's like a big ball of orange light comes creeping out of the ocean and brightens up the earth.

Learning about horticulture is like speaking a new language, only you're communicating with nature. Never occurred to me how grass grows, how trees are planted or how seeds bear fruit. It's really an art. I ate this tomato right out of the ground the other day, yo. It tasted better than a fruit.

We work five to six days a week, twelve hours a day on these large landscapes. They have us clearing the land, preparing the soil with dormant bareroot stock probably for these commercial growers but I can see how profitable the landscaping business is. Even though we're out in the sun all day, I prefer that to cleaning bathrooms or cooking in the kitchen or other housekeeping work around the camp.

"Where's the rest of it?" Bianca asked, disturbed by its abrupt ending.

"Well, I wasn't gonna show you all of it. That's just the part that I thought y'all would want to hear."

"He sounds like a different person," Shashawna said, sounding spooked.

"Maybe all that sun is working on his brain," remarked Harold.

"That's cool," said Christopher, "Because when he starts building houses, he'll be familiar with the whole landscaping process . . . and it makes money."

"I saw you reading some architectural books," Nadira remembered.

"I bought them to send to him. Thought it might keep him motivated."

"I just can't see Deshon digging up dirt or planting trees," said Shashawna.

"Why not?" Christopher asked. "That's big business."

"Ewww, and gettin' all dirty," Bianca said.

"What's wrong with getting dirty?" asked Christopher. "A lot of people have to get dirty before that skyscraper is built. It just doesn't appear. Who do you think is doin' it? You got engineers and architects—"

"Yep, contractors and landscapers," Harold rejoined.

"And all I'm sayin' is, he's gettin' some skills in other areas, but it's relating to what he gonna be doin'."

"That just makes him that much more valuable," Harold added.

"So hopefully when he comes home, he'll be on another track," Christopher said.

"You think he'll get a job planting trees or something?" Shashawna asked.

"No. Ya missin' the big picture. I'm not just talkin' about a job. It's about doing your own thing . . . just like what you're tryin' to do with that lemonade. Empower yourself.

Make your money from what you produce. So if you got the skills or a natural gift for doing something and you like it, and you're planting trees, let's say . . . or catching fish or farming or building a house . . . you turn it into a business. That's the American way. No, really and truly. That's the global way—simple principle. C'mon, what if there were no more jobs tomorrow? What would you do?"

"Rely on your skills," Harold answered eagerly, hitting the bull's-eye—"and feeling inspired by it, too."

"Uh oh," Nadira said, "The man's making good sense."

"That's right! So I'll buy my paper from you, the man who plants the trees," Christopher offered, making deliberate eye contact with each of them. "We're gonna eat the fish that you caught and supplied to the market. Okay, and when I'm ready to build my house, I'm coming to you. And when you want to distribute that lemonade all over the country, I'll be the farmer growing the lemons."

"Picture that," remarked Bianca.

"I can picture it," responded Christopher lightly chortling. "Now how about picturing this? The supermarket around the hood couldn't get the food delivered to the stores. There was a . . . a truck strike or . . . a hurricane or something. What would you do?"

"We'd eat out," Bianca replied.

"And if the restaurants didn't receive their deliveries, then what?"

Passing glances over to the girls, Christopher waited for an answer.

"I guess we would starve," Harold finally said.

"No guess, we would. But if we all relied on our skills and had people like Deshon to depend on who made businesses out of growing our food, building houses and all the other things we need, we'd all be better off . . . healthier, too."

"That's my man!" Nadira exclaimed, hugging Christopher. "He always comes with the truth."

"It's real, yo."

Behind him, Nadira caught a glimpse of Kenya discarding her food tray and waved for her to come on over. Everybody was smiling now.

"Tell him we love him," Bianca said, reading over the note again.

Harold reminded Christopher of the time. The boys gathered their belongings to spend the rest of the lunch break with their other friends.

The sudden thunderstorm threatened to eclipse the light in the old cafeteria. Hordes of students came noisily pouring inside from the school yard. As the darkness descended, the small pool of light overhead cast a faint yellow glow over the area.

"Look, everybody, I want you to meet the next superstar. Take a good look at her now, 'cause she's gonna be worth a lot of money. The girl's got a voice like—name any artist you want— She can blow them right out of—"

"Stop that," Kenya said, cutting her off, lowering her head in slight embarrassment. She was holding a yogurt and an apple juice.

"Don't listen to her, 'cause she's just a little shy, but when she starts raking in the dough, she'll be talkin' then."

"Hi y'all doin'?"

"Oh, I'm sorry. Kenya, this is Bianca. That's Shashawna. Bianca, Shashawna, this is Kenya."

The girls greeted Kenya with condescending stares, hardly able to imagine the soft-spoken girl capable of being the giant talent Nadira claimed.

Kenya noticed Bianca's strikingly pretty features.

"Come on, sit with us," Nadira said, pulling a chair over.

"No, I can't. Camilla's waiting for me," she replied, looking toward the west side of the lunchroom, now getting louder and more crowded.

"Okay, I'm just checkin' with you to make sure everything's on for Thursday."

"You're auditioning for the Spring Idol Search?" Shashawna asked.

"She better be," Nadira said sternly but with a smile, looking up at Kenya.

"What are you going to sing?" asked Bianca.

"Don't really matter," Nadira said. "Just wait. When she opens her mouth . . . not only can she blow like . . . I can't even describe it, *and* she plays the piano like a seasoned pro . . . even better than Mr. Wilson."

"Would you stop that," insisted Kenya, blushing.

"Which reminds me," Nadira continued, ignoring Kenya's protests. "That's what I wanted to tell you. I need your selection by tomorrow."

"Tomorrow?"

"Audition is next week, baby. Ya blink and it's gonna be here."

"There's Leron," Bianca said suddenly, rising up from the table. Appearing even prettier now, dressed in a fitted jean skirt and a midrif sweater, she said, "Be back in a minute."

"When you get over there, tell Nequon to get me a pack of those butter crunch cookies," Shashawna said.

Kenya found it difficult to pull her gaze away from Bianca's stunning beauty. What was Leron doing in the lunchroom at this time?

"So you're ready?" Nadira asked. "Kenya!"

"Hah."

"Are you ready?"

"Yeah, uh huh."

Feeling her preoccupation, Nadira let her go. "We'll talk about it later in the gym."

"Nice to meet y'all."

Kenya followed Bianca's trail, her eyes straining to keep up with Bianca's purple-lavender sweater. *What would she and Leron have to talk about? A girl as pretty as that has to have a boyfriend. Maybe they're just friends. It may not even be my Leron. I'm gonna follow her and see where she's going.*

Thunder rumbled overhead, and the crowds and tightly knit groups became more difficult to get around. She weaved her way around circles of people, trying not to lose sight of Bianca, and bumped right into a girls' back while she was carrying her lunch.

"What the heck?" charged the large girl, catching the drink on her tray before it spilled. She was a tall, plus-size Hispanic girl—who looked white—with a blue-eyed stare that demanded an explanation.

"I'm sorry," Kenya apologized. "That was my fault. I wasn't looking."

Bianca was now out of sight. Kenya walked through throngs of people hoping to find her and soon arrived at her table. Suddenly, she had no appetite.

THE NEXT day, late in the afternoon, a fire drill sent students wildly stampeding out of the Telham Park High School building. Faculty members led their students down Van Buren Street as far as two blocks, snarling traffic. It had been a long, tiring day for Kenya after taking two tests—one in English, and the other in math—and a pop quiz in history.

When the next alarm sounded, signaling the fire drill's end, long lines of students formed, trying to get back into the building. Kenya walked up the back stairwell slowly, wishing for the afternoon to pass quickly, then laughing to herself about the quarrel between two boys occurring earlier that almost turned into a fist fight over a replica watch. Suddenly, a pull at her knapsack forced her slightly backward. Just as quickly, she found herself securely gripped in two strong arms, breaking her fall.

"Whoa, sorry," she said.

"Sorry for what?" a familiar voice said, slowing Kenya to a halt at the top of the landing.

A subtle gasp escaped from her, taken aback by surprise as she fixed her eyes on Leron.

"Where you been?" he asked, a sly smile on his handsome face. "I've been looking for you."

Kenya searched his face and parted her lips to speak, but no words came to her.

"I thought you forgot about me," he said, his dark eyes penetrating hers. With a casual sense of familiarity, he slipped his hand around her waist. "Can I get a hug?"

A little reluctant, she leaned into him. His hard, strong body felt good to her as he firmly embraced her. "Yeah, that's my girl."

The endearment brought a blush to Kenya's face and in an instant, the hurt, humiliation, and unexplained abandonment was all forgotten. She wanted to keep up a nonchalant façade about her, though her heart palpitated at his presence.

"How you doin'?" he asked.

"Good."

"You don't want to talk to me any more?"

Kenya glanced at him awkwardly, jolted by the comment. "Don't want to talk to you?" she echoed weakly.

"I was waiting for you to call me," he said, turning her head toward his. "Hey, what's the matter, you can't look at me?"

"You could've called me."

Widening his eyes innocently, he said, "I didn't know what to think, so I just chilled." He positioned Kenya sideways against the wall, monitoring the oncoming traffic, now dissipating to just a few students.

"Why didn't you just ask? You knew where to find me."

With a dispirited sigh, he averted his gaze and said, "It's not that simple. I didn't know what to say . . . after the way things went down."

Feeling even more confused, Kenya clumsily shrugged her knapsack from her shoulders, noting the time. "I don't care, you still could have called. How do you think I—"

"Forget it, let's just start all over," he said, interrupting her flow of words. "When are you comin' over again?"

Kenya cast a dubious glance at him as she recalled their last encounter. "For what?"

"For what? C'mon . . . how we gonna ever get close?"

"I-I don't know," she replied, capturing a glimpse of his pleading eyes, all the while drawn in by his fragrant cologne.

"C'mon, come by my uncle's on Wednesday."

"I don't know."

"Please."

" . . . It might be hard to—"

"I'll call you over the weekend," he murmured as a slow grin stretched across his face. "Maybe this time we can get something to eat."

At the stairwell door he tried to kiss her. She dodged his lips and he pecked her on the cheek. Kenya didn't offer a definite yes or no.

"A fire drill this late in the afternoon . . . stupid," he said as they began to walk.

"Yeah, right" Kenya agreed.

"Should've just let everybody go home."

"That would have been nice."

Leon abruptly stopped as they arrived in the open corridors on the third floor. "Look at me. I'm going the wrong way," he realized, and immediately changed his direction. "I'll git wit'chu later."

Caught in a web of mixed emotions, Kenya reviewed the exchange in her mind as she drifted back to class. *Why didn't I tell him what was really on my mind? The way he acted, how he tried to jump all over me. Then he doesn't even call to say hello or to see how I'm doing. I should have never let him get away with that. What if I would have—"*

A whiff of his scent, strong and tantalizing, was still clinging to her. A part of her panicked, now aware of the winsome charm he possessed. *He looked so good. And when he touched me. Maybe we did get off to a bad start. Things happen. Now what excuse can I come up with on Wednesday?*

nine

At 3:00pm sharp on Thursday afternoon, auditions for the Telham Park *Idol* Search officially began. An air of expectation charged the auditorium, awaiting the school's most outstanding talent to grace its platform. Students brought all their potential to this moment, accompanying their naïve but heady dreams about becoming superstars.

Kenya sat alone on the front right aisle closest to the window, away from the chattering cliques. *Four minutes, thirty-eight seconds. You can do it. My name is Kenya Robinson, and I'll be performing a song called, I mean a song entitled, "Welcome to the World."* She repeated that line in her head over and over again, craning her neck every few minutes to see if Leron was still there. Kenya had caught a glimpse of him in the beginning of the hour, but she wasn't able to see him; the auditorium now mobbed with people.

Four fifty-five p.m. Kenya had sat patiently through three group acts, five soloists, a female guitarist, four rappers, a poet, and two stand-up comedians. She sandwiched her cold hands between her thighs, humming the melody to her chosen selection in an attempt to keep her nervousness at bay.

The audience dwindled considerably as supporters of the already auditioned exited, their curiosities satisfied. Kenya looked over the small group of remaining students hoping to see Leron. He had never returned.

"And the final contestant," Ms. Kaplan announced, "will be Kenya Robinson."

Uh Oh! God, please let me sing this song right. The walk up to the stage seemed long and lonely. Kenya could feel her insides trembling, her heart galloping in her chest. As she approached the stage, she stumbled slightly, not realizing there were four—not three—steps. Scattered chuckles sounded in the distance, but she was thankfully able to break her fall. She stepped up to the microphone, which was several inches too high. Her face held the look of a frightened kitten as the room fell silent.

"You are a solo performer. What will you be singing?" Ms. Kaplan asked, leading her to proceed.

She lifted herself up on her tiptoes and replied, "I-I'm going to—"

"Adjust the mike, Kenya," Ms. Kaplan instructed.

Kenya looked at the stand from top to bottom and began fumbling with trembling hands to try to lower its neck. She could hear her breath bouncing off the sides of the auditorium walls.

"Pull it straight down," one of the student judges said.

When the mike was level to her mouth, Kenya had forgotten the question. She tapped the mike twice with her hand and said, "T-testing, testing," and backed away.

"Tell us the name of the song you'll be performing," Ms. Kaplan repeated.

When Kenya moved forward, she stepped hard on its base, causing the stand to spring forward. On its return back, her lips brushed past the side of the mike, and it fell to the floor. The loud blast sent several students into gales of laughter.

"That's very rude!" Mr. Hodges, one of the teacher judges admonished, standing up and facing the group. "For the tenth time, we've asked for silence. No comments, no laughter, no distractions. If you can't adhere to these rules, please leave!"

When the quiet of the audience returned, you could hear a pin drop. Kenya briefly looked out into the iron faces of the students and drew in a quiet, deep breath.

"Go ahead, Kenya," said Ms. Kaplan.

"Name of your song, please," said Ms. Bartucci, the second member of the faculty judges.

Kenya cleared her throat and put her hands to her side, preparing to sing. Determined to keep the microphone steady this time, she held the mouthpiece to speak and mistakenly turned it off.

"Um . . . the name of the song I'll be performing is 'Welcome to the World.' "

"We can't hear you, Kenya," Ms. Kaplan said.

Unaware that the mike had been turned off, Kenya strained to raise her volume. "The name of my song is 'Welcome to the World!' "

"The mike is off!" Lazaro Seidman, a stagehand, shouted out from the back.

Kenya looked around, confused.

Lazaro came out from behind the stage, checking for any technical difficulty in the wires. He reeled in the squirming electrical cord, surveying every inch of it right up to the microphone.

In the meantime, Kenya tried not to look at anyone in particular, her palms sweating, her stomach in knots.

A trouble-shooting stagehand everyone called "Denzil" came out to assist Lazaro. "You turned off the switch," he told her as he turned it on. His amplified words wailed out from the massive speakers, sending them shooting across the expanse of the auditorium. Despite the attempts to cover their laughter, the students' taunting came through loud and clear.

"That's it. You have to leave!" Mr. Hodges demanded.

He was ahead of Kenya by about two seconds. She couldn't take the humiliation any longer and was about to leave.

Students filed out, their unrelenting ridicules trailing them. Kenya saw Nadira clearly now, and was pulled toward her gestures of encouragement. When the last of the students left, Kenya felt a thousand-pound-weight relief.

"We apologize for the rude behavior, Kenya," Mr. Hodges offered. "Try to relax, take a deep breath, and proceed."

"Take it nice and slow," Nadira added. She was sitting on the edge of her chair, beaming up at Kenya.

I can do this. I can sing this one song.

Kenya dropped her hands to her sides, took a breath, and exhaled slowly. "My name is Kenya Robinson, and I'll be performing a song entitled 'Welcome to the World.'"

"Thank you," replied Ms. Bartucci. "Will your selection be accompanied by music?"

"Yes, but I'll sing without it today," Kenya replied, looking out into the comforting blackness of the auditorium. Out of the silence, she hummed softly, listening for the microphone's amplification, and adjusted the level of her voice. In a slow and even tempo, with a warm, textured tone, she slid into the groove of the popular tune:

> *"The day you were born*
> *Something in me changed*
> *Looking through your eyes I*
> *Felt new hope"*

She enunciated every word perfectly, her flawless high-pitched voice enhancing their meaning:

> *"The questions I had*
> *They were no longer*
> *My purpose on earth*
> *Came crystal clear"*

As she reached the lower register of the melody, the notes poured out of her like a steady, quiet stream:

> *"Welcome to the new world*
> *In perfect time to*
> *Bring us change*

> *Carrying the torch into tomorrow*
> *The future is where you will reign"*

She made a powerful leap from the chorus to the next verse of the song, holding on to every note with absolute accuracy. Comfortable with her stage persona, Kenya mentally escaped into her imaginary cave, where there were no boundaries. Improvising now, she traveled easily over shimmering octaves, and then changed chords for the last verse:

> *"I'll be the rock*
> *That you can stand on*
> *The compass to lead you*
> *Through life's storms . . ."*

Tears of pride welled up in Nadira's eyes and with every note, sorrow and suffering seemed no more. Ending sweetly, all the judges sprang to their feet, applauding with amazement. Kenya slowly opened her eyes, still floating in the depths of her dream world, and thankfully bowed her head.

"TAKE THIS number and divide it," Kenya muttered to herself while averaging out her three science quiz scores. If she scored only eighty-two, she would be two points from an A for the first marking period, so eighty-eight was the goal. She exhaled thankfully, realizing that mainstream biology was a realistic expectation for the next year.

"Pssss. Kenya, look," said Camilla, pointing at the door.

As Nadira entered the room, students stared in curiosity at the stranger.

"Can I help you?" Mr. Swayze asked.

"I have a message from the office. One minute, please?" Nadira asked, pointing to Kenya.

"Nadira! What are you—"

"YOU ARE IN!" she announced, an excited gleam in her eyes. "You're in, girl!"

"What?"

"The show. You made it! The list is out. Look."

Kenya was stunned as she saw her name in big, bold print.

"You rocked 'em, girl! YOU rocked 'em!"

They threw their hands together in a smacking high-five and then embraced. All eyes and ears were glued to them, and the excitement grew contagious.

"Kenya's gonna be in the talent show!" Camilla blurted out.

"When?" a girl named Madina asked.

"You tried out?" a young man asked, sitting across from her.

"When's the show?" Camilla asked. "I'm coming."

Kenya tried to recall. "It's, um—"

"I didn't even post it yet," Nadira realized, cutting her off. "Everybody's waiting for me now, 'cause they know I got the list. Gurrrrl, you know I had to check it out, even though I knew in my heart of hearts you made it; I wanted to see the official word. And I wanted you to hear it from me first. I am so happy for you," she squeaked, hugging Kenya again.

"The teachers are still talking about it; you should hear them. 'Oh, my God, that girl's got a voice like an angel,' " Nadira mimicked. " 'I've never heard anything like that before.' "

The students around her laughed.

"But I gotta go. Just don't forget the deal we made."

"What deal?"

"Amnesia, have we?" Nadira asked, a teasing twinkle in her eyes. "You said that if you made the audition we were gonna rehearse at my house . . . not that you need to do any rehearsing, as grand as you are, but remember we agreed that we've got to wrap the package just right and make sure you win."

Kenya smiled, nodding in approval.

"Talk to ya later. Thanks," she yelled to the perplexed Mr. Swayze as she shot out the door.

By the time Nadira returned to the main office, she'd found Harold with his friends, and together they sliced through the sea of people waiting at the announcement board.

" 'Scuse us, 'scuse us, please. Make some room . . . we're coming through," said Harold, leading them.

"Yo, yo out of the way!" Zachary and Malik echoed, trailing them.

The crowd swarmed together, stretching and craning their necks to read the list. One girl stormed away crying when she didn't see her name. Another girl screamed excitedly and was so emotionally charged she leaped into her boyfriend's arms shouting, "It's my time!"

Tyrese did a Tarzan-like yell, beating his chest with both his fists. When one girl signaled to the rest of the group that they had made it, a wave of feverish hysteria charged the air, with screaming and shrieking echoing up and down the administrative office's wing.

"Y'all acting like somebody just offered you a record deal or something," said Zachary.

"For somebody here, it just might be," Harold noted.

One young man started singing the words to his group's audition song, and together they began harmonizing, putting on an enviable performance.

"Oh shoot, that girl Kenya made it!" someone said.

"I don't know how she did that," Malik remarked, surprised.

"Who, Kenya?" Nadira jumped in. "Y'all missed it, since you couldn't control the noise. She was the only one who received a standing ovation."

"No she didn't," Harold gabbed.

"Oh yes she did! She blew everybody away."

"Yeah, and my pockets, too," Malik said.

"Not yet," Zachary corrected him.

"What's that supposed to mean?" Nadira asked, with a steamy glare.

All eyes fell in different directions, guiltily realizing that Malik and Zachary should have curbed their comments. "It ain't nothing," Harold answered, with a soft squeeze to Nadira's shoulder.

"Ay, time to move, get to class," shouted Big Mike, a school safety officer, thwarting the celebration.

"What's going on?" another officer, short and chubby, asked.

"The spring idol audition," a girl named Quintana said, gesturing with her eyes at the list. "All those people made it."

"Okay, yeah, I'm happy for you," said Big Mike, "but tone it down and get to your classes."

"We're outta here," said Harold, leading his friends.

"Yeah, I gotta run too," said Nadira. See ya."

"WHAT DO you think about that all-white outfit . . . the long skirt, with white or silver boots? Nadira asked, looking in the window of Hi Esteem, a boutique along the boulevard. They were in route to Nadira's house. "You got the body to work it."

"Yeah, that's hot, but my mother wouldn't be able to afford it."

"You don't necessarily have to buy it. We could get my mother to make it."

"Your mother can sew like that?"

"Can she? All she has to do is look at a style. Huh, people will think you bought it on Fifth Avenue somewhere. Then, we'll just have to buy the boots . . . like those right there, look."

Inside the window were four-inch pointed toe leather boots with diamond-shaped rhinestones extending from the zipper.

"Those are beautiful!"

"I can see you wearing them, Kenya."

"They look expensive."

"I bet you they're not. Spring is coming. Winter clothes are crazy cheap now."

The walk home from school turned into a fun-filled window shopping spree. Dodging in and out of stores, Nadira proved her point as they viewed signs advertising "rock-bottom prices." At one store, the prices were so irresistible they put two sweaters on free layaway.

"HERE SHE IS, Mommy," said Nadira, making introductions.

"I've heard so much about you, Kenya, good to finally meet you," Mrs. Watford said, embracing her lovingly. She was a slender woman, shapely and good-looking. Tall, like Nadira, with shimmery black hair falling freely down her back. "Come on in, sweetie."

The spacious living room was beautifully furnished: plush carpeting, leather furniture, modern window treatments and beautiful art. In no time Kenya caved into Nadira's anxious pleas and belted out a popular song to an audience of three. Nadira's younger brother, Maxwell, had left his computer to hear her extraordinary voice. At the end of the performance Nadira's mother crossed her arms, tilted her head thoughtfully, and pronounced Kenya's musical ability with one word: "Anointed."

For afternoon snacks, the girls forked into succulent bite-size chunks of honeydew melon, cantaloupe, and they dipped strawberries into light whipped cream while flipping through the pages of fashion magazines.

"Kenya, you see that? Cool and glamorous in white."

"Oh, that's real nice," Kenya marveled, looking at a model dressed in an all-white backless dress.

"Add some style and do somethin' different. See what I'm sayin'?"

Kenya turned the page to a fashionable young model wearing sneakers, a long velvet skirt trimmed in lace and a tweed jacket. "Oh, that's hot!"

"And look at her hair . . . parted down the middle in two braids. How simple is that? But elegant at the same time."

"I wear my hair like that sometimes."

"Yeah, you do, but if I had told you to mix and match your fabrics like this girl right here, you would've looked at me like I had three eyes. Sometimes you have to see it on someone else to be convinced."

"Uh huh, I see what you're sayin'."

"Ay, I bet a lot of these clothes come from thrift stores or flea markets."

"That's where I go all the time," Kenya said.

"Are you kidding? That's where you find the best deals."

"And they're all one of a kind."

"Just like you, Kenya. So we're gonna dress you up on the outside to match what you got on the inside. Come on."

Nadira's room was a vibrant two-toned mix of mustard and burnt orange with specks of black accessories.

"This is so nice," admired Kenya, inspired by the decorative balance between youth and adulthood. A framed picture of Nadira as a child, stopped her in her tracks. "Awww, I didn't know you took ballet. You look so cute."

"That was a hundred lifetimes ago."

"You look about seven or eight."

"Think I was what . . . six."

"You're so lucky."

"That's nothing. Everybody takes ballet."

"Not everybody."

"That's because you were taking piano lessons."

"No. I never took any lessons, remember?"

"And how did you learn to play?"

"I told you, I play by ear."

"Well, you didn't really miss much," Nadira rattled off, hoping to downplay the privilege, and then rushed off. "I've got something to show you. I'll be right back."

The ballet picture reminded Kenya of her past—yet not one as colorful as Nadira's. *Where would I have been if my family would have shown interest in my talent?* Her thoughts wondered back to a time when she first began to play notes on the piano. She could play a song by ear after hearing it only once. Relatives and classmates were amazed when she performed impromptu concerts for them, singing and playing with the grace and style of a trained professional.

Her musical ability increased along with her curiosity, and she began to back up her mother's gospel singing in church while experimenting with popular songs and different chords and modulations. Then she began to invent some things of her own—all of this without an ounce of formal instruction.

Broadway maybe . . . yeah, I can see me on a stage with—"

"Look at these," Nadira said, interrupting her thoughts. Dangling between her fingers was a glittering pair of rhinestone waterfall earrings.

"They're *beautiful!*"

"One of my mother's antiques from back in the day."

"Wow, they're heavy," said Kenya, holding them up to her ears.

"She got them from one of those vintage stores in the village, so you know they've been around a long time. Try them on."

"I can?"

"What do you mean? These are the earrings I want you wear with that long, white shirt."

Together they stood in front of the full-length closet mirror.

"Look at you!" Nadira gasped. "I can just see it now."

Turning side-to-side, Kenya envisioned the possibilities, recalling some of her former dreams.

"Okay, picture this. Ten years from now." Nadira's eyes roamed the room in animation, prompting Kenya's rapt attention. She lengthened her upper body, cleared her throat, and positioned her spine so that her voice would flow straight from her diaphragm.

"Here we go. Your first Grammy." Nadira picked up the brass elephant from her dresser with one hand and grabbed her pen with the other to use as a microphone. "First and foremost, I'd like to give thanks to the Almighty . . . for bestowing upon me this most precious gift." She raised her voice an octave or two, attempting to mimic Kenya's voice.

"My mother—the heart and soul of my being—and my greatest supporter, has always inspired me. Dream big dreams, she told me. Believe in yourself when no else does and remain unwavering in your faith." Nadira paused for effect. "I'd also like to thank my producers, my manager, and all the people—too numerous to name at this time—that have made my success possible."

Kenya fell back on the bed in a fit of laughter. "Duh-rama queen of the year!"

"And I'd like to give a special thanks to my longtime friend, associate and advisor, Nadira Watford, who saw the vision early on and encouraged me to make the first step toward it at the Telham Park Idol Search. Thank you, ladies and gentlemen, and may God bless you." Nadira threw kisses out to the imaginary audience, ever so gracefully walking around her room.

Laughing uncontrollably, Kenya fell farther back on the bed, kicking her feet in the air.

"I can see it now, Kenya. Don't you?"

"I don't know. It might be you giving that speech one day, for real. Only it'll be an Oscar, 'cause you are an actress."

"Get outta here. But can you imagine the looks on the people's faces when you sing that song? I can't wait."

"Yeah, but some of the talent at Telham High is really good."

"Kenya, Kenya! I know you just tryin' to be modest, but get real. You know you could sing better than all of them put together . . . in your sleep."

Kenya nodded, acknowledging her opinion, a smirk of pride in her face.

"So come on, let's do this. Stand right here." Nadira positioned her, propping up her head and shoulders. "Come on, no slouching, straighten up, head high and looking out to the audience. I mean, they should get a sense of who you are from the moment you walk out there. Okay, your mike is here, which is gonna already be set up for you. This way you don't have to fumble with it."

"Okay."

"Now look straight out to the middle. I'm the audience." Nadira walked over to the far end of the room, gauging Kenya's appearance like a director. "Okay, you're going to cue the DJ with some kind of gesture, I don't know, we'll come up with something—a nod, or a touch of the mike, whatever. Now begin . . .

"The day you were born
Something in me changed
Looking through your eyes I
Felt new hope"

Nadira could see Kenya was already feeling uneasy by the way she fumbled with her hands.

"Okay, try to keep your body movements and hand gestures to a minimum. I know you may get a little nervous— okay, well, a lot—but practice being still. Go ahead . . ."

"The day you were born
Something in me changed
Looking through your eyes I
Felt new hope"

"It's still showing, Kenya. You've got to smile away your fear. And don't look at me. Look out to your strongest visual focus, somewhere out in the center."

"But when I really get into the song, I tend to look off in different directions."

"That's cool, but only change your focus when the lyrics call for it, like for effect."

"Okay."

"So go ahead."

"The day you were born
Something in me changed
Looking through your eyes I
Felt new hope"

"Good, good, keep going," Nadira trumpeted.

"The questions I had
They were no longer
My purpose on earth
Came crystal clear"

Listening to Kenya's voice, so beautiful, made the hair on her skin rise. Sustaining such glorious sound in an effortless manner seemed amazing to her. Closing her eyes for a brief moment, Nadira was whisked away into the soulful depth of

Kenya's brilliant, smooth sound. She applauded vigorously as her voice trailed off to the end.

"You are incredible, girl! The audience is gonna be shocked!"

"Leron will be, too," said Kenya, giggling. "He's never heard me sing before."

"Leron?"

"Yeah."

Turning her head sideways, she asked, "How do you know him?"

"From school, but we're just . . . kinda like friends."

"Wait. You're telling me you and Leron, Leron Tatum are friends . . . as in going out friends?"

"Something like that."

Nadira tried hard to mask her disbelief and her concerns as well. "So, how did you meet him?"

"He just walked up to me a few weeks ago," Kenya began with a sly glance. "We started talking, went out together and—"

"Hold up, wait a minute. You mean to tell me that you and Leron have been going out?"

"Yeah . . . we went to his uncle's house on um—"

"Tenox Place. That's where he took you?"

"Yeah."

"Was his uncle there?"

"No . . . not exactly."

Nadira darted her eyes around curiously. "What does that mean?"

"This is our secret, right?" Kenya said in a conspiratorial whisper.

"Of course."

"Okay, he took me there and we went down to the basement."

"You did what!"

"Sssssh!"

"Sorry, sorry" she whispered, hardly able to contain her emotions.

"We went downstairs, listened to some music, you know and—"

"Don't tell me you slept with him?"

"Sssssh . . . nothing like that."

Nadira's face folded into an unpleasant frown. "Kenya, don't you think you should be talking to someone . . . you know . . . more like yourself?"

Kenya's neck snapped back. "What's that supposed to mean?"

"What I'm trying to say is . . . I-I been knowing Leron all my life . . . and he's alright, but he gets around with a lot of girls."

"Yeah, he told me he likes to be friendly with everybody."

"Well maybe he's a bit more than just friendly, 'cause I know this girl—"

"Wait, wait. I don't want to hear that. Leron and me . . . we're cool. I mean, he's shy and all that. That's why he's like . . . not open with me in public. He doesn't like people in his business."

"That's what he told you?"

"Yeah."

Nadira looked into her innocent eyes feeling pity, but wanted to shake her into reality at the same time. It was clear Kenya believed his lies. Yet Nadira knew he was one of the cockiest, most arrogant young men in Telham Park High School. *Why did he take her to his uncle's house? And down in the basement?*

"Kenya, listen to me. Leron is not the most honest person in the world. I've known other girls he went out with and I just think—"

"That's your opinion and I really don't care what other girls—"

"But Kenya, he's been known to tell lies, and you deserve better than that."

"How can you say that?"

"I say that, Kenya, 'cause . . . come on, I know him. He looks for a certain kind of girl."

"Like Bianca?"

Nadira paused, uncertain of the right words to say, except to be honest. "To my knowledge, yes . . . they've been seeing each other."

"Who told you that?" Kenya whirled around.

"Everybody knows he's been going out with her. I've seen them together a hundred times."

Kenya's jaw dropped. "Why don't you like him, Nadira?"

"I never said I didn't like him, Kenya. I know him, and I know what a schizoid he can be."

"A schizoid? Oh no," Kenya objected, her eyes turning angry. "I don't believe you said that. And you supposed to be my friend."

"I am your friend," argued Nadira. "How can you say that?"

"Easy, when you can throw that girl in my face?"

"I'm not throwing her in your face. I'm just telling you."

"Why can't they just be friends?"

"Okay, Kenya," Nadira said, softening her tone to settle the angst. "Maybe they're just friends."

"Then why do you jump to conclusions like that?"

"I guess I just didn't want you to get hurt, 'cause Telham guys . . . well not all of them . . . but you gotta be careful who you're going out with."

"Well I don't think he'd be asking me to go out with him again if he was seeing someone else."

"Going back to his uncle's?"

"That's probably where we'll end up, but he said we're gonna do something different."

"Okay then . . . good for you. Why don't y'all get together in school or at McCuller's?"

"What difference does it make?" Kenya snapped. "I told you he's shy."

"Well, there's no reason to get—"

"You talk to Harold, don't you?"

"Yeah, but it's just talk. I'm not really feeling him like that and definitely not enough to make any commitments." Nadira's attempts to enlighten Kenya had somehow gotten tangled and she was clearly upset.

"It's time for me to go, anyway," Kenya said dismissively and took off the earrings.

"We were just getting started."

"No, I had enough for today."

Nadira made impromptu small talk about other things as she walked her out of the building only to receive half-hearted responses. Their laughter had ceased and the mood was spoiled. "C'mon Kenya, I hope I didn't offend you. I was just trying to tell you— Anyway, forget it. We've got more important things to do right now."

Irritation tinged with anger gripped Kenya, though she wasn't certain why. She nodded absently and walked away. "I'll see you later."

From:Nadira@ TelhamParkshs.xle
To: Princess Brixton
Subject: Trouble on the Home Front

Princess,

This just in. Remember I told you about the girl I met who came out of Special Ed who could sing? You're gonna see her in the talent show. By the way, Mommy is hooking her up. Wait until you see her and her voice—it'll make you cry! But check it out.

Leron got her on the Ferris wheel thinking she's the one. But everybody knows he's with Bianca. You won't believe this! He takes the girl to his uncle's house after school where no one can see him. During school he acts like he doesn't know her. I feel sorry for Kenya because she's clueless, and such a sweet person. But check this, Harold told me Leron's got a fifty-dollar bet going on about some girl he's gonna get with next Wednesday. And they were laughing about it like it was a joke. So Kenya was here tonight and told me she's got a date with him on Wednesday. I nearly choked when I put two and two together and figured it out.

Now the show is three Fridays away and I would hate for anything to happen to her. How's she gonna feel after she's been with him and he drops her? It's gonna break her to pieces. And little does Leron know, she's got a big brother—and fine, too! I think Leron would be suddenly missing in action if he ever found out. But speaking as her friend, I can't let this happen to her. Even if she gets mad with me, I'm gonna do what I have to do.

So get this. He agreed to come to the movies with us on Saturday, and he's taking Bianca. Meanwhile he tells Kenya: 'Oh, I don't like public places because I'm a real shy guy.' C'mon, he's a lying schizoid! And he can get away with it because Kenya doesn't run in our circle AND she lives in Bedville.

Anyway, the plan is to show her better than I can tell her. I wish you were here, because who knows what's gonna jump off. Mr. McCuller said hi, and everybody misses you. I'll can't wait to see you.

LYLAS
(Love you like a sister)

"YOU'RE NOT mad at me, are you?" asked Nadira, approaching Kenya in the locker room. Throughout the week, it was obvious that Kenya had been avoiding her at lunch and in gym class.

"Mad? Why would I be mad?" Kenya answered, fumbling through her locker.

"C'mon, Kenya. Be for real."

"It's the only way to be."

"That doesn't sound like the Kenya I know."

Kenya shrugged, absently folding her clothes. "I guess it's just another side of me."

"Not for nothing, but I should be the one who's mad."

"You?"

"Yes. How are you gonna accuse me of trying to put you down? And all this talk about I don't think you're good enough, and I'm throwing Bianca all up in your face? How can you fix your lips to say something like that?"

"Sssshh," Kenya reminded her of the walls around them having ears. "Well, it seemed like—"

"Look, if I thought you to be anything less than my friend, you think I'd be wasting my time? I mean, in all honesty, Kenya, I've got plenty of friends . . . more than I probably need. So it's not like I run around looking for opportunities to connect with people."

A little chuckle escaped Kenya as she watched Nadira throw on the dramatics.

"Princess is my best friend, and she's not here. And I thought I found a new friend. Okay, besides the fact that I want you to win this idol search—but I guess not, if she thinks I'm not worthy."

"I never said that. I just couldn't understand—"

"I was only trying to tell you to be careful, that's all. But from now on, if you're happy, I'm happy. Feel me?"

"Yeah."

"Gotta go. See you later."

Nadira attempted to leave but changed her mind. On all four's she crawled pretending to be looking for something and peeped around to Kenya's aisle and whispered, "You're still my friend?"

Kenya couldn't help but laugh. "Did I ever say I wasn't?"

"Good," Nadira said, exhaling. "Then you can't say no."

"To what?"

"The movies," she replied and popped up. "*Shattered Crystal*, five o' clock on Saturday. I'm paying."

"How did you know I wanted to see that?" Kenya asked brightly.

"Telepathy baby, telepathy."

"You don't have to pay. I have—"

"I said I got it, end of discussion. So let's meet up on the boulevard. Saturday. Four o'clock."

"I'll be there."

ten

*D*uh doo, duh doo, duh doo, was the only sound Kenya could hear in the sanctity of the intensive care unit at Yorkstown Memorial Hospital. Aunt Sophie had been comatose for three days now, following a massive stroke.

"C'mon, Aunt Sophie. Tell me one of those stories," Kenya whispered, bending closer to her ear. "Knocka, knocka . . . Can you hear me? . . . Were those true stories? . . . C'mon, old girl, you can tell me."

Kenya sat in the chair beside the bed, hoping that somewhere deep in the reservoir of her soul, the elderly women could hear her. She longed to speak to the Aunt Sophie she had come to know: The woman. The mentor. The teacher. The friend.

Breaking the eerie calm, Kenya read her homework aloud: "Solve problems fifteen through forty. Read Chapter two, pages forty-two through fifty-nine. Answer end-of-chapter questions. Complete the vocabulary review. Umm, let me see."

Drifting, she stared out the window into the city pondering future scenarios of her and Leron. She followed a ladybug crawling up the wall all alone and wondered where it was headed. Her essay that she'd written seemed drab and colorless, so she consulted a thesaurus to embellish her words. Then, realizing it lacked a logical, coherent flow, she studied a collection of short poems. One of which reminded her of one of Aunt Sophie's adventures. Reflecting, she could hear the matriarch's voice and see her telling the story:

Drifting, she stared out the window into the city pondering future scenarios of her and Leron. She followed a ladybug crawling up the wall all alone and wondered where it was headed. Her essay that she'd written seemed drab and colorless, so she consulted a thesaurus to embellish her words. Then, realizing it lacked a logical, coherent flow, she studied a collection of short poems. One of which reminded her of one of Aunt Sophie's adventures. Reflecting, she could hear the matriarch's voice and see her telling the story:

"Let me tell ya child, the struggle was almost romantic back in those times—not like now. I remember I took this job . . . I was one of those live-in tutors. Worked there for about two years. It was a rich white couple that wanted the children to be tutored and nannied at the same time. My room and board was free, ya know, and they paid me, too. Well, I worked and saved up enough money to send home and to buy me a ticket to London. It was always my dream to ride the Paramount Express.

And there was no more money left after that, not a dime, but I was determined to go anyway. Got on the train and got so hungry my stomach started growling. So I picked up a menu and decided I'd eat the meal of my choice. Got myself good and tight...and that food was something delicious. Well when the bill came . . . I just told the waiter I didn't have any money to pay for it. But being that I was full and strong, I told him that I could work off the meal by washing dishes.

"You were stealing, Aunt Sophie," Kenya said.

"No, I was being honest. I was hungry and I didn't have any money."

"So what happened?"

"You know men have soft hearts for beautiful women, 'specially when they're traveling alone. They did back then, anyway. He let me help clean up the kitchen and I did such a good job he offered me some part-time work, so I stayed on board. I mean, why not? I had a place to sleep, food to eat and all the blues singers came through there . . . Lionel, the Count, Sarah. And a lot of men thought I was Cuban or some kinda Spanish descent because of the way I looked. I never told them no different. But whenever we had the Latins on board, I just served them nicely and smiled a lot. And when they tried to talk to me I answered with one of three words that I knew in Spanish . . . Si (yes), gracias (thank you) and yo no se (I don't know)."

Nodding, Kenya's head leaned sideways, halfway tilting her down. Awakened by the resistant force that pulled her body upright, she immediately noticed that Aunt Sophie was positioned somewhat differently. She stood up, the room feeling new now in the afternoon sunlight. Studying the wave of the electrocardiogram machine, Kenya tried to analyze the beat of Aunt Sophie's heart.

"Knocka knocka," she whispered. "C'mon woman, wake up." A cold, dead feeling crept inside her at the thought of losing her friend. A day without Aunt Sophie was like a day without the sun. Lying so still and complacent, Kenya wondered where she was. Humming, tears formed in her eyes as she stroked her hair, now soft and curly like an infant's.

Back to her work, Kenya read a portion of her English assignment and tried to decide which part of her homework she would tackle first. On reflex, she turned to Aunt Sophie to ask her opinion, but then remembered she wasn't able to answer.

Kenya closed her books and looked over the unfamiliar surroundings. She freshened up the water in each floral vase, making several trips to the bathroom. She gave each of her plants a sufficient dose of water and wiped every individual leaf, giving them a fresh shine.

"Hey!"

Kenya jerked in response at the sudden intrusion. Imani was standing at the door, a look of mystery about her. Grateful for the company, Kenya smiled and mouthed, "Come in."

Imani stared intently at Aunt Sophie as she tiptoed in, barely making a sound. In her hand was a small floral arrangement; a single yellow rose nestled in a bed of green with baby's breath.

"She can't hear you," Kenya said.

"I can't believe it. She hasn't woken up yet?"

"Nope," Kenya replied, shaking her head regretfully.

Imani placed her vase among the other flowers and dropped her bag. She reached over to Aunt Sophie but abruptly stopped. "Can I touch her?"

"Go ahead."

Imani's trembling fingers touched her hand. They both watched the woman who meant so much to each of them. Within the fragile body lay a pillar of strength, a life of many experiences, a staunch optimist, and a believer of miracles.

"Okay, Aunt Sophie, we get it. It's time to wake up," Kenya said, rubbing the side of her face with the back of her forefinger.

"Hey, remember the story she told us about the time she walked out of a jewelry store wearing a hundred-thousand-dollar ring?" Imani asked. "You think she was telling us the truth?"

"Who knows," Kenya chuckled. "She said it looked identical to the ring she was wearing. And when she took it off to try on the real diamond, the lady got confused and put back the wrong one."

"Yeah, and the people were so happy when she returned it, they *gave* her a diamond ring," Imani added. "You believe that?"

"With Aunt Sophie, anything's possible. But if it's not true, it was a good story."

"That's real," Imani recalled. " 'Cause she had me thinking about that story for days."

"I remember seeing her for the first time," Kenya recalled. "She was sitting in the back pew all alone. I asked her if she needed anything, and she started giving me orders."

"Yep, that's her," Imani agreed. "Just as bossy as she knows how to be."

"Huh . . . then you find out she's soft as cotton, tender like a sweet old lady."

"I can just imagine what she'd be saying right now," Imani whispered. "Always telling me not to live so fast. What am I supposed to do, suffer forever?"

"What are you talking about?" Kenya looked perplexed.

"I gotta get out of there."

"I thought you said you were gonna chill."

"We talked about it and we . . . he wants me to move in with him."

"What kind of sense does that make?"

"It's a place for me to live right now."

"In two years, no less than that, you can have your own place. Look what happened to your mother?"

"Different day, different world. I'm not endin' up battered in some shelter."

"Think she thought she would? So why put yourself out there like that? I don't trust it. You're still better off with—"

"No, I'm not," Imani objected. "And now she's talking about sending me to some Job Corp."

"That's good experience . . . and money. Then when you come back, you can go to college."

"And not see Mike for the whole summer?"

"So? He's not going anywhere."

"You don't know that."

"Why don't I? 'Cause if he does, then maybe that tellin' you he's not the one."

"I don't want to talk about it any more," Imani said in a huff. She was getting emotional.

They calmed their conversation, captured by Aunt Sophie's stillness. Tears welled up in Imani's eyes. "When is my day coming?"

"Every day is your day . . . is what Aunt Sophie always says. It's how we choose to live it."

KENYA DIDN'T want to invite Nadira into her shabby home on Saturday afternoon. She glanced out the window every few minutes, hoping to see her coming and meet her outside.

"Pretty nippy out there," Ms. Robinson said, watching a Saturday afternoon movie on the women's cable channel. "Make sure you put a hat on."

Instead of meeting Nadira on the boulevard, Nadira's mother decided to give them a ride to the movies. Kenya scurried around the house, tidying up and making certain that everything looked presentable in case Nadira wanted to come in.

Kenya dashed past Chad, who had just awakened from his afternoon nap, to run up to her room when she was diverted to her mother's room by the ringing phone.

"Hello, Kenya."

"Imani? Whassup. You just caught me. I'm on my way to—"

"You gotta message from Leron," she said, cutting Kenya off.

"I do?"

"He wants you to call him. Something about meeting him on Wednesday."

"Oh, okay, thanks. I'll call you later 'cause I gotta go."

By the time Kenya got downstairs, Nadira was at the door making pleasant conversation with Ms. Robinson.

"You look just like your mother," Nadira noted.

"Lucky for me," Kenya smiled affectionately, putting her coat on. She pecked her mother's cheek and the two girls headed out.

"Too bad y'all are in a hurry," Ms. Robinson said, shivering from the wind. "Come again when you have some time."

"I will. And when I do, would you please sing for me? Kenya told me you have an unbelievable voice."

"Is that right?" Mrs. Robinson smiled, flattered.

"Yes, and I know it's true because I've heard Kenya's."

"For you honey, I'll sing anytime. Y'all have a good time and be careful."

"Bye," the girls said in unison.

THE LONG lines in the crowded Cineplex dwindled down as people moved into their perspective theatres. With popcorn and sodas in hand, Nadira led Kenya toward the upper-level back seats, where her friends were. Next to Harold were two empty seats.

The introduction to the movie came on bold and thunderous as last-minute traffic tipped in. Nequon and Shashawna sat two rows behind them, and two rows below them were other students Kenya recognized.

The soft whispers of the couple seated in front of her, and Nadira's mouth running like water with Harold reminded her that she was alone and not with Leron. The movie's dramatic beginning held her captive but when the fast-paced adventure died down, Kenya heard laughter break out and she looked behind her.

"They are so rowdy," Nadira whispered.

The constant chatter and outbursts continued until they became annoying.

"I don't know who those people are over there with that noise," Nadira said, turning around. "Don't you hate that?"

Kenya gazed in ordinary curiosity and turned further around to steal a glance in that direction and then did a double-take. The young man had a remarkable resemblance to Leron, sitting next to a girl. Confused, she initially dismissed it as her imagination, but there was no mistaking that face. Every time she heard another wisecrack, she turned to look.

It can't be. Leron wouldn't be at the movies. He doesn't like movies. As the film progressed, Kenya's desire for popcorn ceased. Every time she turned, she caught another glimpse of the girl. Finally she was positive it was Bianca. Anxiety rushed through her.

"I'm going to the bathroom," Kenya whispered to Nadira.

"Want me to come with you?"

"No, you stay here and tell me what I missed."

Kenya walked out of the theatre and circled the lobby, anxious and agitated. She re-entered the theatre from the left side instead of the right, and moved up the center aisle, pretending to be lost, then walked up to the top row. She sat in a corner seat eyeballing the young man who was wearing a fitted hat, and she could see his ponytail. It was Leron. Watching Bianca cradled in his arms and stealing kisses infuriated her. *That lying, dirty . . . how could he—this is so embarrassing!* Feeling alone and violated, she looked around, desperately anticipating her escape. *No, I can handle this. I'm just going to play it off and when the movie's over, I'm going to hurry up out of here because if I walk into him with her I'll . . . I don't know what I'll do.*

Nadira sensed something was wrong when Kenya returned. "You okay?"

"Um huh," she replied, taking quick sips of her soda. "What'd I miss?"

"They did a flashback showing how they first met. It was real cute 'cause they didn't like each other then. He had everybody believing he was this snobby rich kid but come to find out—"

Nadira's words faded away as Kenya peered at the movie screen, unable to grasp its plot. Her mind was running in a thousand different directions.

"Ayo!" a male voice called out of nowhere. "Leron!"

Nadira and Kenya looked back at the same time and saw Leron responding to the call, clueless that he had been busted. Without a word, Kenya grabbed her coat and headed out of the theatre. Into the night she ran, gasping for air, talking back to the inner voices admonishing and ridiculing her. She was no match for their sinister power, but she couldn't provide a defensive comeback. Faces swimming toward her grew smug and everything around her—the cars, trees, houses and street signs—seemed to look mockingly at her. The very wind in its whirling fury seemed to taunt and chastise her for her foolish judgment.

That spine-tingling memory leaped alive in her mind: Leron's hands roaming freely over her, sending her throbbing and trembling as she surrendered herself to his trust. She wanted to crawl back into her shell, and she wished that she had never become a part of this new clan of ruthless, dishonest people.

"Kenya!" Nadira called, fiercely chasing her. "Kenya!"

"What's the matter?" Nadira cried, grabbing her arm.

"Don't go there," Kenya replied, pushing her away. "You saw him. So what was this . . . a setup so everybody could laugh at me while he's slobbering all over Bianca?"

"Nobody's laughing at you, 'cause nobody knows . . . but I wanted you to see for yourself what a *dirtbag* he really is."

"But we went out together," she sobbed. And all the nice things he said to me… and calling me all the time."

"That don't mean jack to him! He's a liar, Kenya. Does that look like the quiet, shy type who doesn't like movies? Think about it. Every time he met you, it was always a secret. That's because he didn't want anybody to see y'all together."

Everything looked hazy as her watery eyes clouded her vision. Thoughts of deception and betrayal invaded her, squeezing her chest and choking her. The tears flowed down her cheeks like running water.

"I'm sorry, Kenya. Don't cry, please."

Flushed with shame, she longed for laughter and light. She wanted to call out his name and demand that he appear with an explanation. Only in a nightmare could such a departure from the fantasy of her and Leron exist. With the back of her hand she wiped the tears that had rolled underneath her chin.

"Would I be more of a friend if I had lied? You have talent, you're pretty; you don't need him."

Nadira's words seemed to be coming at her from some faraway distance, echoing in the air around her. With the back of her hand she wiped the tears that had rolled underneath her chin thinking of Leron kissing her, his warm hands, his pleas to be with her. Then the thought of him kissing someone else gripped her, and she walked off.

"Kenya. Kenya, wait!" Nadira cried chasing her.

"I'm gonna call him."

Nadira stopped Kenya in her tracks. "Do you hear what I'm sayin'? The man is a liar!"

Her gaze hardened. "Okay, we'll see on Wednesday."

"No, Kenya, listen to me. Whatever you do, don't go back to Tenox Place. He's trying to make fifty dollars off of you."

"Fifty dollars?" Kenya frowned uncomprehendingly.

Nadira pulled Kenya's open coat together, breathed deeply and braced herself. The cat was already out of the bag and ready to fight. "Listen to me. He made a bet with his friends that he could have his way with you. A cheap fifty-dollar bet . . . and they were all coming to the house to settle it at five o'clock. And you were going to meet him, what, at three?"

Kenya searched Nadira's face, her eyes darting wildly, as she took in the information. She hated herself, this moment, and all the people she thought she knew. "You're lying!"

"You think I would tell you something like that if it weren't true? Why would I want to hurt you like that? Think about it, Kenya. How did I know about Wednesday?"

"Because I told you!"

"No, you didn't," Nadira argued, lowering her voice. "You said you were going out with him again, sometime next week or something like that. And how did I know you were going to Tenox Place? How did I know what time they were meeting him? Harold told me the whole game plan. And look, the guys said you wouldn't do it, but he's the one who called the bet and said you would. They have more faith in you than he does."

Kenya covered her ears, refusing to hear any more. A hole opened up inside of her, making her feel suddenly weak. Aching with tears and a broken heart, she began to run. Looking neither to the left nor the right, she took to the street.

In the same moment, Nadira spotted the car coming fast and the distance was short. "Kenya, NO!"

She reacted to Nadira's desperate call and turned left. The approaching car screeching madly stunned Kenya still, like a frightened deer.

"KENYA!"

The car suddenly swerved around her, barely missing her petite frame, then screeched to a halt. A small, bald-headed black man wearing rectangular framed glasses jumped out.

"Are you crazy? I could've hit you."

"She didn't see you, Mister. We're sorry," Nadira explained, pulling Kenya onto the sidewalk.

"Do you know what kind of accident this could have been?" he yelled, half-stunned.

"I know, Mister. We apologize. She didn't see you. Kenya, you okay?"

Kenya looked off in a haze with tears still streaming down her face.

"What's wrong with her, anyway?" the man asked. "She retarded or somethin'?"

Nadira dismissed his ignorance and attended to her friend, now trembling.

"I'm okay," Kenya said solemnly. "Just leave me alone."

Forced to respect her wishes, Nadira backed off but followed her all the way home from a distance. Kenya walked and cried in the cold. Hurt and frightened for her friend, Nadira was crying, too.

SLEEP DIDN'T come easily for the Robinson family that night. Chad had been out beyond his curfew, keeping

Ms. Robinson from falling into a sound slumber. Kenya wanted sleep to come badly, and escape into a nowhere existence where Leron and all of Telham Park didn't exist. Mali, the youngest, was suffering from a mild earache that kept him dozing in and out of sleep as he lay next to his mother in her room. Morocco's coughing denied him a restful sleep, forcing Ms. Robinson to get up and give him some cough medicine.

The streets outside were silent as the 2am hour approached. Finally sleep, but in a tormented slumber, Kenya tossed and turned, struggling to breathe, lethargy hovering over her, impeding her movement. *Her spirit journeyed into a chaotic dream where she was climbing on a cliff without a safety rope, and when she looked down, she was playing the piano on a subway station platform. In a flash, she moved across mountains and plains below burnt-orange skies in a jungle safari. Down below her, the grassy waters that gushed up along the narrow banks turned to splotchy mud, yet the overwhelming desire to feel it engulfed her.*

Suddenly the sky turned dark—a purplish black. The flow of the muddy waters turned to a rough, rugged terrain. Then, in a twinkling of an eye, a big, shapeless object hovered over her. Kenya could feel her body effortlessly being lifted in mid-air and carried off, as if she were sailing smoothly through the waters. She finally reached a clearing point where bright stars shimmered and many people reached for her from an open pit of activity. As she moved toward them and her body plummeted downward, into its mouth. In a split-second her descent stopped, and a pair of firm hands lifted her out of the death-plunging leap.

Partly conscious, Kenya felt a painful stinging in her throat and an overwhelming urge to cough. The burning sensation around her chest felt heavy. Sirens rang out peculiarly behind mysterious voices. Someone was screaming. Dogs were barking unusually loud. She was placed horizontally on a soft cushion, below a sky of blackness.

The loud screaming crystallized as she could sense it coming near to her. "Lord Jesus, Kenya! Can you hear me?"

Kenya wanted to acknowledge her mother's cry, but her voice was too flat, like someone was choking her. She tried again, and a gurgle came out. Her trembling body was shielded from the night chill with a heavy blanket. Colorful, blinking lights seared through the darkness and the volume of the sirens increased.

"Can you hear me, Kenya? Wake up!" Her mother continued hysterically. Four bodies hovered over her, and she was vaguely able to see the waves of green in their uniforms. A mask was placed over her face while another set of hands moved around her wrists and throat. In her peripheral vision, she could see the colorful fiery flames, and at that moment, they appeared almost beautiful to her.

"Vital signs are good," a deep male voice said. "She's gonna be okay."

The fire came to the Robinson household like a thief in the night, quiet and unexpected. The heat in the parallel strands of the electric wires that Chad had taped up a few weeks before had ignited. The flames caught on to the walls, then the rugs, and crawled up the draperies before making their way to the sofa, living room furniture, and then into the kitchen. As the heat began to rise, there were crackling, popping sounds, and glass breaking, which startled Chad awake. He first thought to call 911, but the nearest phone on the kitchen wall had melted to an unrecognizable glob from the intense heat. He snaked his way through the mass of smoke toward the bathroom, quickly drenched a towel and rushed ahead of the flames into his mother's room. He shook her into consciousness and grabbed his two young brothers. Thinking fast, he lifted the window and tossed the crying boys out.

"I gotta get Kenya!" Ms. Robinson cried, coughing huskily.

"No, I'll get her. You get out!"

"No!"

"Get out, Mommy, I'll get her!" he commanded, tussling with her and then finally shoving her petite body out of the window to safety. Through the black smoke, he could hear sirens in the distance. In a mad panic, his adrenalin flowing, he crouched down low and dodged the flames to get to the stairs. "Kenya!" he yelled. "Kenya! Get out!"

Fighting the stinging in his eyes, he yelled so loud he began choking from the heavy soot blanketing the air. In his mind he imagined he heard Kenya's piercing cry. "Help me, Chad! Help me!" Desperate to rescue her, he wrapped the wet towel around his head, closed his eyes and leaped toward the towering flames. Out of nowhere a pair of heavy hands pulled him back suddenly. Turning around, he saw vague images of three large men walking out of the black smoke in fire suits, holding axes. Another firefighter sent a stream of water gushing through the house.

"My sister's upstairs!" he cried.

Two men took off to save Kenya, and the others helped restrain Chad. "No!" he cried, fighting with all his might, but he was no match for the strong figures. "Let me get my sister!" he pleaded as he was dragged to safety. "KEN-YA!"

Within a few minutes, a seeming eternity to the terrified family, a firefighter walked out of the black smoke and burning flames, carrying Kenya's limp body. Slowly regaining consciousness, a circle of faces surrounding her, she realized she had woken up from a bad dream to a tragic reality. Force-filled streams of water coming out of fire hoses gushed onto the house, but the flames were leaping uncontrollably. Right before her eyes, her house at 65 Tetherball Street—the one she'd grown up in, the one full of life, laughter and their meager possessions—was disappearing right before their eyes.

"Mommy!" Morocco cried. "It's gonna burn down everything!"

"I know, I know, but we're alright," she said, coughing wearily.

"Tell me this isn't happening," Chad said in a cold, ghostly voice.

Hearing him, Ms. Robinson grabbed him and pulled him toward her. "You're safe, we're alive. That's all that matters."

"Good thing you saw that smoke, man," said their neighbor Reginald, to Conway, who was standing next to his bike. He had discovered the house on fire riding through the block and called 911 from his cell phone.

"What happened?" some woman asked.

"How did it start?" a male voice inquired from behind.

"We've got to get y'all some place for the night," an EMS worker said.

"Jesus!" Ms. Robinson cried out as the wood departed from the frame of the house and the pieces began falling to the ground, the heat radiating over the scene. Firefighters continued to work breathlessly, a stretch of hoses crowding the area.

Kenya felt herself weakening, watching the remaining portion of her house being eaten by the tortuous flames.

Holding on to her children, Ms. Robinson wept. Their life-long possessions were now reduced to ashes. No clothes. No food. Nothing. Kenya trembled as she was being lifted into the ambulance. When the door slammed shut, like some bad nightmare out of a horror movie, it sent her body into a shivering panic.

eleven

"The Department of Social Services told me they were staying in a temporary shelter downtown," Mrs. Watford told Nadira when she picked her up from school on Tuesday afternoon.

"How's Kenya?"

"The woman said she was doing okay."

"People will tell you anything on the phone," Nadira mumbled, dissatisfied, then reached into the box of clothes in the back seat that her mother had picked up from the church. "Think she's telling the truth?"

"Sounded pretty genuine to me," Mrs. Watford replied, driving off. "And what would be the point of lying?"

"Why couldn't she give you more information?"

Mrs. Watford tossed a glance over her shoulder and said, "Sometimes people don't want their whereabouts exposed at times like this."

"Why not?" Nadira asked, inspecting the clothes. "We're not trying to be nosy, we're just concerned."

"I know . . . but dealing with the shock of it all is sometimes hard for people."

"And we have money and clothes to give them."

"How much more did you collect in school after I spoke to you this afternoon?"

"I don't really remember, but all together I've got . . . seven hundred."

"What! You collected that much?" Mrs. Watford beamed proudly.

"Actually, I collected six-something, and the school put in the rest. The secretary gave me the letter to give to the family."

"You did good, girl."

"I did alright," she said dryly, having expected more from the one-thousand-plus student body and more than one hundred teacher staff.

Still rummaging through the box, Nadira saw T-shirts, sweaters, jeans, underwear and pajamas. "These clothes are nice, Mommy."

"I pulled out the best stuff from the bunch, and the underwear I bought from Value World." Her mother's words settled in the back of her throat as she thought, *My heart goes out to that family. Kenya's such a nice girl, and that voice—my goodness!*

"So we're going go see them now?"

"Baby, we can't just walk in on them unannounced. We would have to call first and make sure they're up to having any visitors."

"But look at all this stuff we have for them," Nadira said, sliding back into position in the front seat.

"I know, but I wouldn't take a chance going down there until I knew for sure we were welcome. We don't really know them. I mean, I did meet her mother that one time . . . from a distance, but—"

"I told you, she's a real nice person. She would love to meet you. And remember, the Spring Idol Search is the Friday after next."

"I'm sure they have more important things on their minds right now. You can't really be expecting her to perform."

"Oh yes I am!" Nadira exclaimed. "She needs to, Mommy. I mean . . . it doesn't change anything that's happened. Plus, it's a chance for her to win five hundred dollars. We can get her ready, buy the outfit, the boots and get her hair done. Then all she has to do is show up and sing."

"You're going all the way with this, I see?"

"Well, I was planning on helping her, even from the beginning. She's such a talented person, Mommy, and so sweet."

"Feeling guilty still?"

"Well . . . yeah, that too."

"Don't be so hard on yourself for—"

But I'm the only one cheering for her Mommy and a person like that deserves a chance."

I know your intentions are good, baby, but sometimes—"

"Remember, you told me how you had to be strong when Great-grandma died?" Nadira asked and clutched her arms to drive her point through. "And how you had to pick yourself up even though you didn't want to. And how you cried for a hundred and thirty-something days straight."

"Um hum," she replied, catching a glimpse of her daughter's pleading eyes. It made her so appreciative of Nadira's kind, generous spirit. Slowing down, Mrs. Watford was preparing to parallel park when her mind rushed back to her time of grief. A respectful pause came between them, giving her a moment of reflection. "C'mon let's, go," she said abruptly when she turned off the car. "We'll call over there and see when we can visit them."

Nadira looked carefully through her entire room— the dresser drawers, underneath her bed, the closet—and selectively chose any items, new or gently used, that she could add to the box for Kenya. She collected a pair of jeans, a denim skirt, an all-weather jacket, a designer belt, and a blouse. She found a pair of white sneakers that she had only worn once and wiped the scuffmarks clean with a powder cleanser. She noticed three pairs of shoes in her closet that she rarely wore and added them to the collection. The suede boots were cute, but she could never seem to match them with any of her clothes, so she wiped over them with a damp towel and neatly placed them back in the box.

"Nadira! Come here," Mrs. Watford called urgently.

"I just spoke to the people at the shelter," she informed, her face pleasantly gleaming. "We can go see them this evening."

MOTHERS AND children moved in and out of the small, cramped lobby of The Clarion, a renovated shelter that had once been a hotel on the south side of Telham Park. From the looks of some of their hard-beaten appearances, they had been homeless for some time.

"You're visiting?" the guard asked suspiciously. He was a tall, thin, older black man with a head full of silver hair.

"Yes. We called earlier," replied Mrs. Watford. We're here to see the Robinson family."

"Robinson, Robinson," he mumbled, picking up the phone. "Yes, ma'am, that would be room 314."

A million thoughts ran through Nadira's head, her eyes narrowly focusing on the families coming back and forth. One of the children spilled a milkshake on the floor making an ugly mess that everyone seemed to ignore. Women trailed by nonchalantly with strollers, clumsy bags and absent-minded children lagging alongside them. *This is what the Grisham House is like—or worse, she thought.*

"Sign in here, please," the officer directed, approving their identifications. "Elevator's down the hall there to the left."

A group of teenagers tore out of the elevator that seemed too small to contain them. Nadira and her mother darted suspicious glances at each other, as they were crowded into one corner by others who had rushed in behind them. The elevator moved in crippling slow motion to the third floor— long enough to feel the despair, sense of abandonment and acute discomfort of being displaced out of one's home.

The doors opened to a long, narrow corridor that reeked of pine. Splotchy beige water-stained walls were marred with stray marks and fingerprints. The combined sounds of music, television and loud voices weaving in and out of rooms whirled in the hallway's echoing acoustics. As they neared room 314, the harsh sound of steel locks unbolting shot through the air. Suddenly, Ms. Robinson appeared, a drawn and worn look about her turned bright when she saw her visitors.

Nadira dropped her packages, falling into Ms. Robinson's welcoming embrace.

"It's good to see you."

"So good to see you, Ms. Robinson. How are you?"

"We're hangin' in, thank God."

"This is my mother."

"Nice to meet you, again," Mrs. Watford greeted. "Holding on is all we can do sometimes."

Ms. Robinson sighed heavily, nodding slowly. "Yeah, it's been rough . . . but God is good, 'cause all of my children are with me."

"He's merciful," Mrs. Watford praised.

"Yes, indeed."

"We were so sorry to hear about this, Ms. Robinson."

"Call me Natalie, please."

"How's Kenya?" Nadira asked. "She didn't get hurt—"

"This child has not slept since this happened," Mrs. Watford interjected, hugging her daughter close to her.

"No. Kenya's alright, baby. Just suffered a little smoke inhalation, that's all. They kept her in the hospital overnight, but she's fine. Just . . . well, you know." Her voice settled to a whisper. "Come on in."

The room wasn't so bad—the basic, standard stuff: Two queen-size beds, a small table, a dresser, a television, and two chairs occupied the space. Kenya's two little brothers sat on one bed, watching television. On the other, Kenya was lying down, her body facing the window, draped with muted blue curtains.

"Looking at something in particular out there?" Nadira asked, carefully inching toward Kenya.

Kenya sat up, coming alive in disbelief. "What are you doing here?"

"Came to see you," Nadira replied, embracing her. "I would have been here sooner, but we couldn't find you. You're not mad at me, are you?"

"No," Kenya replied softly. She looked tired and very sad. "You don't have to feel sorry for me," Kenya said, beginning to cry.

"Oh course I feel sorry for you! I'm your friend. Wouldn't you, if this were me?"

"I guess . . ." she sniffled, shrugging lamely. "Pitiful, right?"

"How can anybody with a voice like yours be pitiful? I'm the pitiful one, remember? I can't do anything but shuffle papers."

There was something different going on inside Kenya. In her voice, lower and steadier now, Nadira felt intractability in the resolve of her words. She could also read her thoughts. "You think I feel sorry for you for another reason, don't you?"

Kenya didn't respond.

"Yeah, I do feel bad about what happened to your house, but that's the only reason I feel bad. I did what I did on Saturday 'cause I didn't want to see you get hurt." Nadira caught herself as she realized their mothers could hear them, and lowered her voice.

"I told my mother," Kenya admitted.

"You did?"

"Ms. Robinson, I'm sorry," Nadira pleaded. "I just wanted Kenya to see for herself 'cause she wouldn't listen. Anybody who would do something—"

"I tried to tell her," Ms. Robinson agreed, jumping in. "It's a small thing, and he's a heartless person. The world is full of them. One of these days when she sees the light, she'll wonder why she ever gave him the time of day. But now she saying she doesn't want to go back to that school."

"What!" Nadira said, rising to her feet and then falling back to Kenya's side. "You can't leave Telham High. You don't have any reason to."

"I told her that," Ms. Robinson concurred.

"How are you gonna deprive us of all your talent, your laughter and . . . YOU! And what about me? I'm still there."

A fresh, new layer of tears slid down Kenya's face, and she turned toward the window.

"She's doing so well in her classes," Ms. Robinson lamented. "I wouldn't want to see this progress she's made disrupted. See, I'm not concerned with anything else, but she is. But you can't run away when things happen."

"Gotta stand up to it," Mrs. Watford added. "Every trial makes you stronger. Every kick is a boost, and no matter what, baby . . . you've got to move on. I know this probably seems like the worst thing that ever happened to you, but it's not. Look how God spared your life. He's got a plan for you. So pick yourself up and make the first step."

"Yeah, Kenya, like singing in the show next Friday. Don't let this stop you."

Kenya shook her head adamantly and fell back on her pillow.

"Why not, Kenya?" Nadira cried, seeking support from Ms. Robinson.

"What have I always told you, Kenya?" dovetailed Ms. Robinson. "Your voice is a special gift from God, and I know He wouldn't be pleased if you didn't use it. Situations gonna come, baby, some far more serious than this. I tell you that all that time, and it's hard . . . but the darkest hour comes right before the daylight . . . and you have to be awake to greet it."

"Tell me you're gonna still sing on Friday," Nadira pleaded. "I want so badly for everyone to hear your voice. We've got everything all worked out for you. So all you have to do is show up . . . and sing."

There was no response from the shy introvert.

"I'm not playin', Kenya. And look what we brought for you," she continued, trying to keep her focused and attentive.

As Ms. Robinson pulled out the clothing, a look of gladness spread across their faces.

"Oh, there's something else we forgot—compliments of Telham Park High School," announced Mrs. Watford.

When Ms. Robinson read the letter, announcing what seemed to be a small fortune, she pressed the letter to her heart. "My God . . . we are so grateful. Look at this, Kenya."

Leaning into Ms. Robinson, Nadira whispered, "Please make sure Kenya makes the show next Friday, please."

"You're gonna listen to your mother and go out there and sing, right?"

Kenya rose up reluctantly. "I can't promise you . . . but I'll try."

Nodding sorrowfully, Ms. Robinson said, "I know my child, and her heart is more bruised over that boy than her house burning down."

Kenya closed her water-filled eyes, and a stream of tears coursed down her cheeks. Nadira rubbed her arms, comforting her. "C'mon, I know you feel bad. I mean, the guy was tryin' to take advantage, but look. His plan didn't work. I'm telling you, he's nobody and even less of a nobody for what he did."

"They were laughing at me because they think I'm retarded and—"

"Stop saying that! There's nothing retarded about you. Look what you've got. You don't need any validation from those skeezers. And that's all the more reason why you've gotta get up there on that stage."

"No. . . I just don't feel like getting up there and—"

"It's not about what you feel. We don't feel like going to school every day, but we go, and we learn and we grow . . . right? Go out there and make those skuzz buckets feel smaller than the filthy ants they are. Then we'll see who has the last laugh."

In walked Chad, diverting everyone's attention. "Hello," he said, being bum-rushed by his two little brothers.

"We got new clothes!" shouted Mali. "Look!"

"This is my oldest son, Chad," Ms. Robinson said proudly.

"Nice to meet you," he nodded, and did a double take, an admiring gleam in his eyes, looking at Nadira. "Oh, yeah, that's right," he recalled. "I met you the other day at the house."

"Where have you been?" Ms. Robinson asked, her tone turning authoritative.

"Had some things to take care of."

"I've been waiting for you since four, and it's seven-thirty now. You know I'm worried when you tell me you're—"

"C'mon, Ma, chill with that," he grimaced, issuing a plea with his eyes to halt the admonishment and not embarrass him in front of company.

"We had turkey burgers for dinner," Morocco informed him. "We bought you one, too."

"You did?"

"Chad!"

"I hear you, Ma. What's up, Boobie," he said, glancing over at Kenya. He could see she had been crying, and his face went blank, his eyes etched in concern. "What's the matter?"

"Nothing. She's all right," Ms. Robinson answered and cut her eyes over at Mrs. Watford, nodding worriedly. "Please, don't get him started," she whispered. "When he found out about that boy, whew! Tore out of here like a madman. He's crazy about his sister, ya know."

"I can see that," said Mrs. Watford, rising up out of the chair. "We're gonna get out of your way now, and leave you to your evening . . . but we'll be in touch. And if there's anything you need, just let us know."

"Thank you so much . . . for everything," Ms. Robinson said, gently embracing them both. "And you're welcome to come see us anytime."

"Kenya, I'll be waiting," Nadira said as they walked out the door. "Don't let me down."

"GRAB SOME of these," Nadira commanded the group of boys in Mr. Ramsey's office. She rolled several boxes of non-perishable food to the door on a large dolly. A local food company had just delivered them to the school.

"Why didn't you call me down, I would have brought it up," Harold asked, hauling up a box.

"No big deal," she said, gesturing to the school janitor's dolly. "Mr. Chapman packed it all up for me, and I took the elevator up."

She turned to walk away and continue working, but then turned back, remembering two things. "Zachary, make sure you take this back down to Mr. Chapman when y'all are finished, and here . . . give this to Mr. Ramsey when he comes back." Nadira did a double take when she noticed Leron talking with the group.

"What's he doing here?" she muttered to Harold, her pretty brows furrowed.

"Helpin' out."

"Why's he wearing those dark glasses? There's no sun in here. What, can't look at hisself or somethin'?" Recalling his despicable actions, she quickly grew heated at his mere presence. "Leron!" she called out. "You dirty—"

"Chill with that," Harold urged.

"What do you mean? I've been trying to run up on him all week."

"He's busy right now. Leave him alone."

"Leron!" she called again. She saw a concerted effort among his friends to feign distraction.

"What's all of this?" she asked, tossing suspicious glances at all of them.

"They're workin' on something over there," said Harold, hoping to wind her down.

Nadira circled around him and moved toward Leron. Harold grabbed her by the arm to pull her back.

"Get off of me!" she said, snatching her arm out of his grip.

"C'mon, Nadira, leave him alone."

"No. I'm collecting donations, ya heard? Let's see how generous we can be," she blurted sarcastically.

Harold pulled at her again, trying to move her away from the circle of boys that formed a wall, shielding Leron.

"Donations, donations anyone . . . for the Kenya Robinson's tragedy," she said, trying to squeeze her way through them. "I'm sure you know who she is. Her house burned down and her family lost everything! C'mon now, I know you have at least fifty dollars you can donate to the cause," she fired out, tossing a look of disgust to all of them.

"I don't want to hear dat," Leron mumbled.

"What! You don't want to hear it?" she spewed loudly, "Is that what you said?" Zig-zagging across the line of boys, Nadira tried to get in. "But you were listening loud and clear in that basement, right?"

"Dira, c'mon," Harold urged, pulling her away.

"Oh, now you're gonna ignore me, huh? Took advantage of that girl like that. It's all good, though, 'cause you're gonna get yours!" she fumed loudly, pacing like a tigress around them, her eyes cold and narrowed. "Wait till I tell Bianca."

"Betta stay outta my business!" he said.

"What's that? You threatenin' me?"

Harold grabbed her by the waist and lifted her off her feet, but she kept on talking. "Why don't you take those glasses off and man up? Bet you don't know nothin' about that, right? That's why you look for girls like Kenya. If you were a real man—"

Harold moved her out of the office, but her voice still echoed down the hall.

"Shut up!" exclaimed Harold. "Everybody's gonna hear you!"

"He's wrong!" she lamented. "And why you protecting him? You know what he did was—"

"I'm not protecting him," he replied, cutting her off. "I'm just tryin' ta keep things civil."

"Civil? How can you be civil when you're dealing with the uncivilized? He's a skeezer, an animal! Or maybe I shouldn't say that, 'cause animals have feelings. Then he's gonna stand up . . . in *my* face. And how come you didn't say somethin'? That girl and her family could have been burned to a—"

The bell rang, drowning out the rest of her words, and instantly the halls were filled with students. Harold didn't try to interfere with Nadira's anger; she was delivering cutting dialogue and gaining speed.

Traffic was sparse on the stairs, and her passionate words became even louder. "Would you shut up and let me talk to you!" Harold had to shout over the din.

"Oh, now you're telling me to shut up," she said. "Lookin' out for ya boy—"

"Tone it down, Nadira!" he demanded, stopping abruptly. Then he backed her into the stairwell corner. "You know why he's wearing those glasses?"

"Yeah, 'cause he's a punk!"

"C'mon," he said seriously, glancing around. "And keep your mouth closed on this."

"Why I have to keep my mouth closed? He was blabbin' to all his friends, talkin' about—"

"You're gonna listen to me or what!"

Nadira turned her face toward the wall, quiet for the first time.

"Somebody went to work on him."

"What?"

"Yeah, I think it was that girl's brother. Found him on Monday night and tuned him up."

"Wait a minute, you mean—"

"That's why he's wearing those glasses. Leron was comin' out of his buildin' and they cornered him. One dude started beastin' on him . . . busted up his eye and some of the rest of him, too."

"You lyin'!"

"Nah. That's why he's been staying in Mr. Ramsey's office for the last few days. His father wouldn't let him stay home."

"Why would his father make him come to school like that?"

Harold shrugged uncertainly.

"Okay, but why do you think it was Kenya's brother?"

" 'Cause . . . people were sayin' the dude was singin' while he was washin' 'im. You know like," Demonstrating, Harold punched his hand with a closed fist, "You . . . wanna . . . play . . . games . . . That's my blood! . . . You ever look at her again, it's over!"

"No!"

"It's what I heard."

Open-mouthed and bug-eyed, Nadira paused, and then exhaled heavily. "So he's been hiding all week."

"You know he don't want nobody to see him like that. That's why I was tellin' you to leave him alone. 'Cause he already got his. Trust and believe . . . he won't be going nowhere near her again."

Nadira chuckled, feeling satisfied as they walked through the crowds on the second floor. She had never known justice to be so swift, or gratification so contenting. "So you think I can get a donation from him now? Or is it too late?"

They looked at one another and busted out in laughter.

"Youz a hard nut to crack, girl."

"Aay . . . you get what you give. Oooh, I see Mr. Perrigno. He's got something for me. I'll catch up with ya later."

"Cool."

twelve

March was turbulently transitioning into spring, and weather conditions were unpredictable. One day was so beautiful, with temperatures warm and welcoming, people had begun to expose their tattoos. Teens loitered on the streets, basketballs hit the outdoor hoops, and vehicles began cruising the streets with open windows.

Then unexpectantly, on a Tuesday afternoon, a snow blizzard caught everyone by surprise. Big, thick snowflakes fell from the gray sky, sending everyone running for cover.

Kenya and her mother stepped cautiously through three inches of accumulation to get to Yorkstown Memorial Hospital. When the news came that Aunt Sophie had regained consciousness, Kenya immediately put her troubles aside—seeming so small in comparison—and went to see her friend.

Aunt Sophie was sitting up reading a book, fresh-faced and her hair groomed when they entered her room.

"What took ya'll so long?" she asked, removing her glasses and eyeballing them. "You know you can't keep the old lady waiting . . . busy as I am."

"Good to see you," Ms. Robinson greeted her warmly, extending her hands. "How you feelin'?"

"Feelin' pretty good, thank the Lord."

"Aunt Sophie, you scared me," Kenya said, gently hugging her.

"What's there to be scared about? Tomorrow's not promised—'specially in my condition."

"Don't talk like that," she said, suddenly overtaken with emotion. Feeling her eyes well up with tears, she looked away, toward the window.

"Uh oh, what's the matter?" Aunt Sophie asked, transferring her gaze to Kenya's mother.

"Nothing," Kenya replied. "Heard you ate a good lunch this afternoon. Oh, and I bought you some fresh fruit."

"Would you tell this girl she can't keep nothin' from me. What's the matter, now?" Aunt Sophie asked again, reaching for Kenya's mother's hand.

Kenya turned sideways while her mother told her of the tragedy.

Aunt Sophie's eyes fell on Kenya, her heart sinking as the words resonated off the dull walls. "I knew there was a reason for me to come back. Lost your books, too?"

"Everything," Kenya replied, her troubles showing on her crumbling face.

"Good thing I kept your work."

"Huh?"

Aunt Sophie pointed her eyes toward the closet. "Go into my pocketbook and take out that white envelope, the plain one."

Kenya unfolded a crinkled sheet of paper, immediately recognizing her own handwriting. It was the uncompleted essay that she had begun to work on some weeks earlier.

"Much better than the last draft . . . just need some minor fixing . . . a little more color won't hurt, either. Go ahead and finish it."

Kenya stood quietly, reading Aunt Sophie's comments, her handwriting faded and jagged. This provoked an onslaught of new tears.

"Sit here, child."

Kenya averted her eyes away from Aunt Sophie's, hoping to mask her emotion.

"Feel like the world is closin' in on you, don't it?"

"Um hum."

"Just opening up for you, baby."

"Can't believe this is happening. All my stuff and—"

"Why can't you believe it?"

"I didn't do anything to deserve this!" Kenya cried.

"And you think the next person it's gonna happen to deserves it?"

Kenya shoulders slumped and she sighed.

"No," Aunt Sophie continued, "But that's the way life works. The sun shines on the just as well as the unjust. It's what the good book says. And the rain works by the same principle."

"But why?" Kenya lamented, a fresh layer of tears streaming down her cheeks. "Why?"

"If we knew why, it wouldn't be a question, now would it? Since it is, we just gotta bear it. But you, little angel . . . things are just beginning for you."

"I keep telling her that," Ms. Robinson offered.

"But where we gonna live?"

"HE'S gonna provide. Doesn't HE always? You're not living in the street. Sleepin' under a bridge. Never went a day without a meal, right?"

"No," she replied lamely. Somehow mere subsistence didn't satisfy Kenya today, and it didn't justify the experience in her mind.

"Think about how your mother's feeling. It's breaking her heart seeing you this way."

Kenya paused in thought, her stomach churning in confusion. "I have to use the bathroom," she said, breaking away.

"Let her get it off her," Aunt Sophie whispered to Ms. Robinson. "She'll feel better."

In Kenya's absence, Ms. Robinson took the opportunity to tell Aunt Sophie about the other news that had upset her. Aunt Sophie listened attentively, showing no reaction. When Kenya returned, she looked refreshed and composed.

"Now that's how I like to see you looking," Aunt Sophie said, smiling.

Kenya assisted her as she tried to shift her weight.

"Thank you, baby, that's better." Aunt Sophie looked out of the window as if she were evaluating the sky, the snowfall freckling the windows. "So what? You fell off of a horse. Feels like the end, doesn't it? But it's not. Why don't you sing something for me."

"I don't feel like singing."

"You're gonna deprive me? I told you . . . you don't ever know when the suitcase is gonna be packed for good."

"Don't talk like that."

"Sing for me, then, and I won't have to."

Kenya began fumbling with the flowers they had brought to her. "Like these?"

Ignoring her question, Aunt Sophie said, "You can't feel like this but for so long. You gotta get out there and sing. Isn't that show at school coming up soon?"

"Friday after next," replied Ms. Robinson.

"I don't want to go back there," Kenya sulked.

"Ooooh . . . want to sit around feeling sorry for yourself instead?"

Kenya turned away in frustration. "I don't understand why everybody's pressuring me. Look at what happened."

"That's exactly why we want you to keep moving," Aunt Sophie said, releasing a series of coughs. "Don't you know moving through the storm is far better than . . . anticipating the damage. When you're moving through it, you gotta chance to come out on the other side. Sitting still . . . it's gonna take you alive. Look around you . . . right now all you see is what you don't have, what you lost. That's nothing, child. You can always get that stuff back . . . and get it back tenfold. But look at what you *do* have."

"Where? I don't see it."

Aunt Sophie leaned her head sideways in thought, her eyes as glossy as ebony pearls. "HE gave it to you when HE woke you up this morning. It's called opportunity."

"I'm not feelin' it."

"Or maybe what you are feeling . . . might be called fear. What'd I tell you about that?"

Kenya looked over toward her mother, who obviously wanted Aunt Sophie to have the floor.

"Come on now . . . tell me what it is. If it's fear . . . you know what I taught you. C'mon, say it with me."

"False . . . Evidence . . . Appearing . . . Real."

"There you go. Can't be scared, baby. All you have to do is open your mouth. The sound gonna come out. See . . . the prize in your life don't come without pain. It's a hard thing, but it's true. Experience is gonna give you some clarity. But until then . . . oh, you can't see through the murk right now. That's why you got old heads like me around. My bones . . . they dance to your delight."

Kenya was silent, musing on the profundity of her words. She could tell Aunt Sophie was getting tired. She set her open Bible on the nightstand.

"Look . . . I want to be empty when I leave here," she muttered, perking up again. "All that I am and all that I have shall there become new possessors of. Take your pain baby . . . and turn it into power. Few in life get the chance to meet their moment. Now I want you to sing in that show on Friday, hear me?"

Ms. Robinson then presented Aunt Sophie with a beautiful bowl of grapes, strawberries and blueberries. "Here it is. 'Specially for you, Ma'am."

"Well would you look at this," she said, admiring the colorful blend of the fruit. "Why don't you turn the television on? Watch a movie with me and share some of this delicious stuff."

They comforted themselves with an old black-and-white musical, laughing and conversing. Obliging Aunt Sophie's request, Kenya graced the room with her angelic rendition of "Amazing Grace" and repeated it over and over again.

About halfway through the movie Aunt Sophie's voice was giving out, and her eyes grew heavy. "I want you to check on that gal for me, Imani . . . 'cause she needs somebody to—"

She drifted off in mid-thought. During a commercial break, Aunt Sophie began humming a musical jingle and perked up momentarily. "Hmm, musta dozed off . . . and don't you forget to finish that essay now. HE didn't rescue you for nothin'. Keep your head up . . . and look to the—"

She dozed off into a nice sleep as visiting hours came to an end. Kenya and her mother slipped out quietly, leaving her to rest.

"IMANI, it's me, Kenya."

"Where are you calling me from?"

"My mother's cell phone. They gave us a free one so we would have some communication."

"How's everybody?"

"We're okay, trying to adjust. How about you?"

"Ay . . . I'm doing what I have to do."

"Meaning?"

"I was hoping Aunt Sophie would be able to go home and you would feel better so I could see you at work."

"No, she's doing better but still not well enough to go home. Maybe next week."

"It'll be too late then."

"Why?"

"Because I'm leaving on Friday."

"Imani, no!"

"I -can't - take - it - here."

"You don't know what you're saying. You've got a roof over your head—"

"It's more than just having a roof, Kenya. You don't understand."

"Maybe I don't. But you can't explain how running away, to God knows where, with no money, no job, no diploma, is the right thing to do."

"I just wanna live my life. A string of mothers and fathers—I've had enough! You don't know some of the things I've been through."

"That's all the more reason why you should hang in there. You could come stay with us, but look . . . we don't have a place to live."

"Mike is looking out for me."

"And what if he turns out to be trouble?"

"He won't."

"You don't know that! A guy is the last person you want to put your trust in, especially now."

"Well, I'll just have to take my chances. Come Friday, I'm out!"

A long pause ensued.

"Kenya. Kenya. Can you hear me?"

"I can hear you."

"Are you crying?"

"No."

"Yes you are. I can hear it. Don't do this to me."

"I've lost everything . . . now you're gonna—"

"You're not losing me. I'll keep in touch. Besides, you're gonna be so busy singing, you won't even remember—"

"I'm not singing."

"Why not?"

"I'm feeling a certain way right now and it's too much."

"Are you crazy? You better get up on that stage—"

"No, no. I've got a lot on my plate and now you're telling me you won't be there to hear me."

"It doesn't matter. As long as everyone else hears you. Now you're feeling like me . . . sometimes you've just had enough."

"It's not the same," Kenya said.

"What do mean? With a voice like yours—"

"Singing in front of a bunch of strangers without my best friend, whose wants to run away from home 'cause she can't have things her way is not exactly thrilling for me. At least you have a place to live. So there's no reason—"

"And you have your family," argued Imani. "Let me tell you something. I'd rather live on the street with my family than live in a *palace* with strangers."

"How you ever gonna have a family . . . or anything, if you keep running?"

"Because I feel like . . . eventually I'll find a place that makes me happy."

"You're not gonna find that in a place. Maybe not even your family. That's gotta come from you."

"Listen to you. You have your family, you got your health, and a gift from God, so you don't have any excuse for throwing away a good opportunity. I mean, and I understand how you feel . . . *to a degree*. Sometimes you've just had enough.

Silence inched between them.

"You still there? Kenya. Kenya."

"Imani."

"What?"

"I was just thinking. What if . . . if I sing in that show on Friday, will you stay?"

"C'mon Kenya . . . don't put me out there like that. I'm ready to go."

"Like Aunt Sophie says, it's not about what you want, but I'm serious. If you stay, and come to the show, I'll sing."

"I'm not gonna make you a promise like that."

"Then I'm not gonna do it."

"See,. now I'm sorry you even called me."

"No, you're not. And by the way, Aunt Sophie told me to check on you, which is one of the reasons why I'm calling. 'Check on that gal, Imani,' she said. Probably knew just what you were planning to do. You know you can't pull nothin' over on her."

"That's what she said?"

"I lie to you not!"

"She's scary sometimes, ain't she?"

"You could look at it that way, or . . . you can look at her as an angel watching over you, especially when you're about to do something really stupid."

"Huh . . . let me think about it."

"What's there to think about? Yes or no? Tell me now."

"Give me some room . . . I'll call you back—"

"Now Imani, tomorrow's not promised."

". . . alright, I'll be there."

"You promise?"

"Promise. But if you don't show up and sing . . . I'm gone!"

"Bet."

thirteen

Kenya shifted uncomfortably on the bar stool chair, stealing glances at parts of her face in the dressing room mirror. She had been sitting still for over an hour, having her face massaged, poked and brushed. Tyra chattered nervously with Imani while applying the last coat of mascara.

"Akile's sounding good," critiqued Imani. She had been present during the sound check earlier. "But she can't touch Kenya. I'm telling you all those—"

Tyra frowned at Imani as a gesture for her to cut any talk about what was happening on the stage.

"Ah, wonder how I would look with blonde highlights?" Imani mumbled, changing the subject.

Traffic dodged in and out of the dressing room in urgent haste. Kenya ran her French-manicured fingers along her nylon stockings to stay calm. With an audience full of people, including her family, and Aunt Sophie in her heart, she had abandoned all thoughts of Leron and was focused on getting through tonight's performance.

Pleased with the make-up work, Mrs. Watford said, "Time to get dressed."

Kenya put on the waist high blouse with keyhole drop sleeves; the form fitting cotton skirt, trimmed with leather details; the leather ankle boots; and then the jewelry. Six hands assisted Kenya, shaping, smoothing, checking, and ensuring that she was perfect.

"Diva Deluxe!" Nadira shrieked, calling attention to the crowded room when they were finished."

"You are gorgeous!" remarked Tyra.

Observers in the room stood back, equally amazed.

A truly stunning Kenya trembled as gusts of applause filled the dressing room. She gleamed in milky white from head to toe, accessorized in a rhinestone necklace, earrings and a matching bracelet, feeling more glamorous than she had ever dreamed. Turning her head from side to side, she marveled at her hair, swept up in a regal bouffant, glittering with sparkling sheen.

"The winner's supposed to shine," Mrs. Watford said, still primping her.

Imani looked upon her friend's spellbinding beauty with teary-eyed pride.

"Twelve and a half minutes," Nadira announced nervously, mindful of every fleeting moment.

Kenya's heart took off in a ferocious pounding as everyone prepared for her entrance. Her fingers trembled as she reached for a tissue to absorb the moisture building up in her hands. Glancing in the mirror at every opportunity, she spoke to herself. *Those people out there are no different than the church congregation. Sing the song like you do at night. Pretend like nobody's watching, just sing. You can do it!*

An entourage of people escorted her up the staircase to the side entrance of the stage, capturing the attention of everyone who laid eyes upon her.

For the first time she felt empowered, possessing her God-given gift, which she was ready to share with the world. Thoughts about her so-called learning disability, her poverty, and her imagined unattractiveness had all vanished. People no longer appeared as big as she had once imagined them to be—untouchable, incomparable, and unapproachable. They were just like her, human beings doing the best they could do, being the best they could be, and using their gifts selectively.

"Our next contestant," Melford Ingram, the up-and-coming comedian who had been selected to emcee the show, announced, "The maestro of words, a man ahead of his time . . . always coming atcha with fire-spitting truth . . . you know him, I know him, we love him . . . ladies and gentleman . . . here he is . . . show some appreciation for Jonathan Mackeby, better known as 'Divine.' "

"I'm so happy you're here, Kenya," Nadira said above the thunderous roar of applause. She was anxiously hopeful for her friend. "You're gonna win tonight, I can feel it!"

"It's okay if I don't . . . it's a miracle that I'm even here. Just pray that I don't bomb."

"Yeah, right," Imani said, hearing her words.

"Would you tell this girl something," Nadira said, trying to make light of her fear as Jonathan's words came between them:

"I close my eyes
In search of the truth
My unexplained behavior
Troubled from my youth

My talent is wasted
My days come and go
I sit back and listen
What history of self
Do I really know?

So bad I want to change
Just don't know how
With so many in darkness
Who GOD can I turn to now

I wish for magical things like wings
That'll one day make me fly
Soaring through the madness
For the things I believe, and be willing to die

I'm small, paid little
Short changed and hostile
Dodging bullets on a daily
I turn to drugs and the alcohol bottle

I don't understand
So I press upon my Father
For answers to this bondage
That makes a man scream and holla . . ."

"He's good," someone said, as they digested the message of his words.

"Kenya, it's packed out there," Nadira said, peeping out. "I want you to remember to look out above the crowd."

"She's gonna be fine," Mrs. Watford said. "Don't make her more nervous. You're not nervous, Kenya, are you?"

"Not really . . . maybe a little."

"This is your show," Nadira said, grinning. "You're gonna win this. Look up, go within yourself . . . and win that prize!"

The panic was creeping; Kenya could feel it. The ground beneath her seemed to move, though she was standing still. Her hands felt icy, though she was burning up inside. Kenya thought of a quick escape. She wanted to flee, but a stern voice inside her insisted she remain calm.

"Can we get a word from Kenya Robinson, the soloist whose about to take center stage?" Raul asked, holding the video camera on her. "How does it feel?"

Kenya turned and nodded, plastering on a smile, but no words came out.

"She feels as good as she looks," Nadira spoke up for her. "And as you can see, she looks bee-aut-iful!"

At that moment Aunt Sophie's words began to speak to her. *Go on out there and sing. Sing with everything you've got, baby. Keep your head up high and I'll guide you, 'cause my bones—they dance to your delight. You'd better get out there and sing, Kenya—"*

"Look over here," Tyra said to Kenya, patting the beads of sweat forming on the bridge of her nose. "Now close your eyes," she instructed, touching her up with a new layer of the rich copper powder.

In the darkness, Kenya prayed fervently. When she opened her eyes the anguishing terror had subsided and the applause signaled the end of the poetry reading.

"We rockin' up in here tonight, y'all!" Melford's voice boomed, as the audience roared in excitement. "No place for the sandman on this stage! Ay, looka here," he spoke loudly, struggling to be heard above the noise. "All I can say is . . . it's gonna be tight. Everybody's a winner here tonight!" The audience applauded again. "Okay, okay, okay . . . for the final performance of the talent search competition we have a solo artist . . . a fine young woman . . . performing for the very first time on the Telham Park High School stage."

Nadira slipped her hand into Kenya's and gripped it tightly. "Break a leg, girl."

"Y'all give it up . . . for Kenya Robinson, performing . . . 'Welcome to the World.' "

The mix of the lights and the velvety curtains sliding slowly over the stained floors gave the otherwise unimpressive stage a wink of stardom and glamour. The effects transformed the stage into a mystical wonderland as dry ice machines shot out streams of white smoke. Applause beckoned, the crowd waiting for the popular song everyone loved.

Appearing out of a cloud, poised and beautiful, Kenya gleamed as the prelude to her song began to play. Scattered applause built up to a roar as she cascaded to the microphone. As the smoke cleared, the auditorium had become a galaxy, and a feeling of calm washed over her. Kenya closed her eyes and hummed along with the prelude, then launching into a soul-wrenching vibrato that brought the audience to complete silence.

Opening her eyes, she remembered Nadira's words and looked above the sea of faces and out to the center. She envisioned Nadira, moving her thin fingers with a feathery gesture, prompting Kenya to let the words flow:

> *"The day you were born*
> *Something in me changed*
> *Looking through your eyes I*
> *Felt new hope"*

Warm applause rushed forward immediately as the surprised audience was struck with her flawless vocals, coming out with an effortless, warm, soulful timbre:

> *"The questions I had*
> *They were no longer*
> *My purpose on earth*
> *Came crystal clear"*

Singing brilliantly, Kenya held the audience at rapt attention as the power in her voice reached them. She moved easily into the chorus, demonstrating her impressive vocal range and inflection along with facial theatrics and subtle hand gestures, further dramatizing her performance.

> *"Welcome to a new world*
> *In perfect time to*
> *Bring us change*
> *Carrying the torch into tomorrow*
> *The future is where you will reign"*

A long wave of applause rolled through the crowd. Her powerful voice began to expand toward the second half of the song, and when she drove into the second chorus, she began to improvise. She sang to the pain of deception, to the tragedy that she and her loved ones escaped, to the future for which she now felt hopeful. Her voice rose higher and higher as she threw out notes to every corner of the room. The audience let go with wild applause.

"I'll be the rock
That you can stand on
The compass to lead you
Through life's storms"

"They'll be no turning back
In route to"

On the edge of their seats, the audience sat breathlessly, in awe of her vocal range. Slowly and passionately, Kenya's voice ascended into a powerful high C.

"D-E-S-"

Then she made a tremendous leap into a high D with uncanny precision, piercing the air like a shooting star—

"T-I-N-Y"

Electrified, the audience rose to its feet thunderously clapping, screaming and cheering. Kenya opened her eyes and confronted her moment. Before her stood a room full of adoring fans that had fallen in love. She held the note, amazing the crowd, and then swooped down to a perfect ending with an immaculate trail-off:

> *"And there's where*
> *You'll live all*
> *Your dreams"*

Appreciative of the adoration—and thankful for an outstanding performance—Kenya pressed her right index finger to her lips, extended it out to the audience and graciously bowed her head.

⋆ ⋆ ⋆

The hour was punctuated by the sound of ancient old church bell. Beyond the sunset, the fullness of the moon shone luminously on the rushing waves in an ocean of the netherworld. White gulls glided overhead, obeying a call from a highest order. And the one star—in a treasury of stars—in the north corner of a transitioning sky burst into brightness. On a journey bound for glory, Aunt Sophie slipped into eternity.

⋆ ⋆ ⋆

"Did ya'll hear what I heard?" shouted Melford, "Ladies and gentlemen we have to speak the truth . . . That was an EXPERIENCE!" The audience responded with another round of mad applause. "Yes, yes! . . . If I wasn't here, I would have never believed it . . . Judges . . . I hate to say it . . . y'all got some serious decision-making to do."

Backstage, the room was filled with congratulations, laughter and cheers as Kenya was deluged with praise.

"What a gift!" she heard from several people.

"You have a glowing, amazing voice!"

"You rocked it!"

"That was beautiful!"

"Awesome talent!"

"Wonderful performance!"

"Yes girl! Yes!" yelled one hefty-sized girl, reaching for Kenya with a great big hug.

Together, Kenya Imani and Nadira embraced. "Mission accomplished!" cried Nadira.

FINALLY, the moment of truth arrived. Contestants lined up across the front of the stage, silently hoping to be the chosen one. The air was charged with excitement as Melford called off the third-place winner. Second-place winner. "And the first-place winner is . . . hold on y'all," he said, fumbling to open up the envelope. "Uh oh," he looked around, blank-faced. "Who y'all think it is?" he teased. "No, I'm just playin', I'm just playin'. Ladies and gentlemen, faculty members, parents, students, friends, friends of friends, the first-place winner in the Telham Park High School *Idol* Search—whose going to walk away with a nice little piece of change, I might add—goes to…" And then he purposely fell silent.

"The winner is . . . Kenya R o b i n s o n!"

The audience went wild, roaring with crazed intensity as Kenya stepped to the center of the stage in disbelief. Now on their feet, they shouted and screamed and extended their hands along the foot of the stage, some trying to get onto the stage. A chant of "Encore!" resonated in the distance as she was presented with a huge bouquet of white lilies and Sterling roses. Security escorted her mother to the stage with Chad trailing behind her, and together they cried; only this time they were sweet tears of joy.

"FROM DUST we came. To dust we shall return, and in between we live life." With a tremulous timbre, Reverend Cornelius eulogized, "Death has no untrammeled sight, it's target-perfect, purposed and appointed—a mystery far beyond the understanding of mere mortal men . . . Anna Mae Nichols, also known to some as Aunt Sophie, was a performer in her own right, a mother to many, salt of the earth, but first and foremost . . . a woman. A beautiful soul lent to us for only a season. But in her attendance there are those that she touched and those who will continue her legacy. She wasn't exempt from the many troubles that come with the rising of the sun, and the thorns of life had wounded her some. But she triumphed above it all, a staunch optimist no matter what the day brought . . ."

On the platform of the altar, in an oak mahogany-finished casket, lovingly adorned with white Casablanca lilies, surrounded by elegant candlelight, the dearly beloved Aunt Sophie peacefully lay. With her creamy skin casting a glow, as if in a normal sleep, she looked far younger in the muted lights of the elegant church. And placed between her fingers was a Sterling rose from Kenya's congratulatory bouquet.

Inside the packed church, perfumed with the fragrance of fresh flowers, white broad silk bands hung respectfully from the balcony and across the pulpit. Sympathy flowers ranging from the simplistic to the extravagant were displayed proudly, with large Peace Lilly plants lined up from the altar and spilling down the aisles.

"Anna Mae Nichols," the Reverend warmly chuckled, "could be very sharp-tongued when she wanted to. The Bible says . . ."

Kenya caressed the pocket-sized poem written by Aunt Sophie and distributed to attendees as a keepsake. Feeling heavy-hearted, the stories Aunt Sophie had told her rushed through her mind, but the memories of her "life lessons" made her smile, offering a welcomed reprieve.

"The book of Ecclesiastes, Chapter 3, tells us to every thing there is a season," Reverend Cornelius continued. "A time to be born, and a time to die, a time to weep, and a time to laugh; a time to keep silence, and a time to speak; a time to break down, and a time to build up . . ."

Seated at the piano now, Kenya had prepared a special tribute to the woman who'd grown so dear to her heart. It was a sweet melody that arose out of her grieving heart. In a soft, moving tone, she sang:

"Thought it was a dream
Till my eyes opened up
In the flesh you appeared
With an angel's touch

Embracing me with loving arms
When sorrow gripped my heart
You made clear the way
For a brand new start

Your eyes,
They're watching me
Your eyes
They speak to me
Forever in my heart
You'll always be"

Kenya's glorious voice rose through the silent, open air as people reflected on their pasts, the present and their unknown tomorrows. There were no outwardly open or frantic outpourings of mourning, but mostly silent reverence; soft moanings and an occasional fit of crying coming from Imani, who was seated prominently on the first row.

"Eyes burned like the sun
Could shine through the rain
Found light in the dark
Easing away my P-A-I-N

Your eyes
They're watching me
Your eyes

They speak to me
Forever in my heart
You'll always be
My G-U-I-D-E . . ."

AT NOON, the casket was carried out by six distinguished church members to the sound of the adult choir singing "Precious Lord," one of Aunt Sophie's favorite spirituals.

The crowd lingered in the jam-packed foyer, awaiting the organization of the procession. The commendations on Kenya's performance came in numbers, following hugs and kisses and handshakes from total strangers. When Kenya looked back, remembering where Aunt Sophie rested, the empty church glowed from the wave of candles lit.

"That was an incredible performance," a tall, black middle-aged man said, appearing out of the crowd suddenly.

"Thank you," Kenya said. A shy smile was the best she could offer, and she started to move away.

"Mansey William's my name."

His tenor voice aroused Kenya's curiosity. "Um, I'm Kenya Robinson."

"Do you perform often?"

"Not really. I sing in church sometimes."

"And in school," Imani jumped in. "Not only does she sing, she's the *winner* of the talent competition we had at the school last week."

"That means I'm talking to the new Telham Park Idol."

"That's right," replied Imani.

"Any aspirations on singing professionally?"

"I've thought about it," Kenya replied nonchalantly.

"Seriously?"

"Once or twice."

"Maybe you should. Not too many unique sounds out there. Are . . . your . . . parents here?" he asked, looking over the crowd.

"My mother is."

Mansey reached into his pocket and handed Kenya a business card. "Three-Score Entertainment. It's my new record label, and I'm looking for artists. If you think you might be interested, give me a call."

Imani stood in wide-eyed shock while Kenya read his card. A member of the church came between them and whispered a few words to Kenya.

"Don't forget that," Mansey reminded her as he moved away. "And just in case you lose the card, you can always reach me at the station, WKTR."

"Oh my goodness," Kenya said shyly. "I knew I heard your name before . . . and you'll remember me?"

"How can I forget the name, Kenya? It's one of the most beautiful countries in Africa. And besides," he grinned, "even if I forget your name, I could never forget your voice. It'd be nice to hear it again."

"Girl," said an elderly woman gripping her arm, wearing a reddish wig and glasses, and walking with a cane, "You know you can sing!"

Behind her came others with warm regards for her performance and remarks of sympathy. Soon, people were beginning to make their way outside to get in their cars to lineup for the procession.

"You think he's really serious?" Kenya asked, looking poignantly at Imani. They were waiting on the street for the church van to drive up.

"He's the head of Three-Score Entertainment, and a huge radio personality, c'mon Kenya, do you think he approached you because he didn't have anything else to do? And he wants to speak to your mother, *yes*!" Imani shrieked quietly and then began to laugh.

"You alright, what's so funny?"

"I ain't goin' nowhere now . . . 'cause youz about to blow up! I'm stayin' right here 'cause we're gonna be rich!"

At the thought of the possibilities, Kenya quietly laughed with her. "But Imani, what was he doing here?"

"His grandmother, the woman that raised him. She and Aunt Sophie were best friends."

"I never knew that."

"Yep. And you know what Aunt Sophie always says, "Don't ever turn down an opportunity to be kind to someone—"

"Because you never know where they may take you," they chorused.

THE PROCESSION inched slowly down Telham Boulevard. A gentle woman with a great big heart was to be joined by other great ones returning home. The prolonged silence wasn't altogether filled with gloom, for the many thoughts of Aunt Sophie rang out loud, bold and joyful. Mourners recalled her sometimes girlish laughter along with her ear-bending stories strung from the past and lessons for the future. They remembered her sobering efforts to find compliments in any little task anyone performed. Such a treasure could never be considered a loss.

fourteen

At nine fifty-four a.m. Saturday morning, the dampened street from a twilight downpour was drying by the bursting sun and cool wind. Ms. Robinson checked her watch as she, Kenya and Chad walked hurriedly up the cobblestone walkway to make their 10 o'clock appointment in the quaint town of Ridgemont. Inside Ms. Robinson's canvassed shoulder bag was the overnight express package containing the letter from the attorney's office in charge of Aunt Sophie's estate.

The three-story brick house had been converted to the offices of Davenport & Myers, Attorneys at Law. A chubby white woman with a big smile courteously greeted them. She offered them refreshments and seated them in leather chairs inside the office.

Stephen Myers was an older African American gentleman with a slightly hunched back. He wore round black-wired glasses, donning a gray suit with a navy bow tie. "Ms. Robinson, Kenya, uh . . . and your name, young man?"

"Chad. Kenya's brother."

"Okay, Chad. Good to meet you all," he said, shaking their hands. He pulled out a document and looked at it, his eyes perusing the pertinent points. The silence of curiosity loomed in the air. "You were asked to come here today for what we call a bequeath hearing." His head had a tendency to wobble when he spoke. "Anna Mae Nichols had prepared what is known as a living will, which entitles family members, or whomever she may choose, to be the beneficiaries of her assets."

Kenya turned toward her mother, frowning with questions.

"That includes all of her valuables, all of the things that she possessed at the Crestfield House."

"When did she do this?" Kenya asked.

"Uh . . . a few months back. You see, Ms. Nichols had prepared for her departure in many stages, and she'd call me from time to time to make changes to her will. That brings me to the purpose of your attendance here. Anna Mae Nichols' most valued asset is a piece of real estate . . . that has been bequeathed to ah . . . Kenya Robinson. She is of course underage . . . but it can be entrusted to her guardian until she reaches the age of twenty-one, at which time the property will become officially hers."

"What are you—" Ms. Robinson looked over at Chad to her right and then Kenya to her left with glazed eyes. "Saying to—"

"What I'm saying is Anna Mae Nichols willed her house to Kenya here."

"Wait a minute, what house?" Kenya asked.

"The house she once lived in here in Ridgemont. It was many years ago . . . of course, before she became ill. She never wanted to sell it, nor have any strangers occupy it. So she kept it. Here, look at this and show it to your mother," he said, handing Kenya a manila envelope.

She opened up the smaller envelope first. Inside was the silver key clasped onto the chain that Aunt Sophie always wore around her neck.

"The key you're holding is actually the original key to the front door of the house when it was first built . . . some time back in the thirties."

"It is?" Kenya asked vividly recalling the way she fondled it.

"Yes. Looks like she had it finished in sterling. Held onto it all these years. It's a good piece of property too, needs some work . . . but it's a great asset."

The handwritten page attached to the official beneficiary form read:

> Everyone leaves something behind on earth when the journey ends, whether it is conscious or unconscious: a child, a piece of jewelry, a dream, a recipe, a philosophy by which to live, a picture frame, and sometimes their hope. To you, Kenya Robinson, I leave my key. It is but a symbol representing the many doors that will open for you, but also the key to a home for you to comfortably dwell, where you may find purpose, be prosperous and where you will always have peace.
>
> Eternal love,
> Aunt Sophie

RECEIPT OF BENEFICIARY OF ESTATE

Estate of Anna Mae Nichols, deceased

I hereby acknowledge receipt of the following described items from Steven Myers, administrator of the Estate of   Anna Mae Nichols   , deceased,

The residential property located at   1811 Madison Street   ,

Signed and sealed this 1st day of March, in the year 2011.

_____

(Name of Beneficiary)

Witness   Date

_____

"All of the deceased's estate has been accounted for," Mr. Myers said to Ms. Robinson. "Once you've agreed, you'll need to sign these papers we've drawn up for you."

Among the three of them, they asked a thousand and one questions, astounded by the mind-boggling news. After Mr. Myers put all their concerns at ease, the Robinson family exited the office the proud inheritors of a new home, in a new part of town, ready to begin their new life.

BEDVILLE seemed but a distant memory as Kenya scanned the immaculate block of Madison Street in Ridgemont Hill, a forty-minute bus ride away. Holding her mother's hand with Chad walking next to them, she viewed the regal structures of attached brownstones with wide stairs and massive stoops. She admired the distinct uniqueness of each of them and noticed how the turrets raised on some roofs towered above others. Then she came upon it—1811 Madison Street.

With a choice of doors to use, they entered the house from the street level. A narrow staircase leading to the second floor flanked the small entrance hall. Daylight crept into the living room, and a set of French doors opened up into the dining area.

"Look at the size of this room," Ms. Robinson said.

"Huh," Kenya gasped, pointing to the fireplace, flanked by built-in bookshelves on both sides. The open, dusty space felt warm. She immediately envisioned oddly shaped ceramics gracing the mantelpiece.

"These floors are original," said Chad, bending down to get a closer look.

"Look at this," Ms. Robinson pointed, stepping into the dining room. Its stately interior was enhanced with high ceilings and original moldings. "Imagine us eating in here."

Such a sense of style and taste—just like Aunt Sophie, Kenya thought, running her fingers along the strong, sturdy walls and moving into the kitchen. The vintage ivory-and-sage-colored cabinetry extended around the room above the formica countertops and a deep double sink. Much like Aunt Sophie, the house was full of color and personality. Wherever Kenya's eyes fell, she couldn't help but smile. "Is this really ours?" she asked.

"Yes it is," replied Ms. Robinson.

"Let's look at the bedrooms," Chad said, leading them upstairs.

The second floor was comprised of three large bedrooms. The first one Kenya walked into she immediately claimed as hers. It was an inviting space, welcoming new beginnings. With an imaginary eye, Kenya saw a queen-sized bed, a fluffy white comforter with several lines of white and silver pillows, and thick, plush navy-blue carpeting surrounded by navy walls. She envisioned the white draperies and silver-framed pictures. It bore an uncanny resemblance to the picture she'd dreamt about time and time again in her mind.

The simple bathroom next to her room was small and had the original fixtures in it, including a claw-footed bathtub.

"This is a whole lot of house," Chad said, running up to the third floor. "It's gonna take the rest of our lives to fix it up."

"One room at a time," Kenya said, moving toward the large window that faced the backyard. She looked down into the bed of weeds growing in the large backyard and then looked up into the muted pastels of an afternoon sky, now understanding why blue is called the optimistic color. *Hey there, Aunt Sophie. How are you doing up there? Resting well, I know. Me? I'm doing fine, just like you said I would. Thank God for you.*

ON SATURDAY morning the Robinson family spent the very early hours sifting through loads of clothes and households items that had been donated to them. They worked diligently in anticipation of receiving their new bedroom furniture, scheduled for an 11:00 a.m. delivery. With Chad's help, Kenya's room was spotless—windows washed, floors waxed and new window blinds.

Sitting in the corner was the trunk she had been given, filled with novel items, accessories, and books. Kenya removed the antique silver frame that she had hand-picked to display her first creative writing essay in—of which she received an A. She admired the way the leaves on the inner rim boarded the page, making it appear as if the paper had been cut that way.

Every line had been inspired by the colorful stories Aunt Sophie shared about her life, which were often times embellished, but who cares. It made for good reading. 'Tap into your creative well to ensure the reader enjoys a "tasty" experience,' she would say.

Kenya envisioned the essay on the wall above her desk or a place that would enable her to see it from her bed. It would be a reminder to keep building between the storms that would come in life. When you see a success story, Aunt Sophie once told her, always know that something, someone or some part of a person had to die so that the dream could live. Kenya was then drawn to read the essay once again.

THE DREAMS I OWN

Underneath the covers, my private escape, the music and the magic pull me in like a river flowing upstream. Eyes wide open or tightly shut, the privilege of the darkness provides me the canvass where only "I," the artist, can color the journey.

The covers are a landscape of boundless horizons. No rules or limitations, restrictions on my creativity, or invented obstacles must I endure. A rich and famous vocal Diva or a nurse, a classical pianist or founder of a music school—any one of which I may be with the broad stroke of my anointed brush.

My thoughts turn into song. The blanketed walls absorb the soothing drone of heavenly melodies and then I am transported. To places unknown, raw emotion pours out of every note as I segue from R&B or jazzy blues to sweet sympathetic gospel that harkens unto the angels. I wonder. Yeah, underneath the covers there are no boundaries to my dreams. Inside the darkness comes a light that illuminates my human essence, an unearthly beauty that distinguishes me as a unique creation.

—Kenya Robinson

ABOUT THE AUTHOR

JENNIFER BURTON, a native of New York City, has always been intrigued with multicultural interaction. While teaching in a Brooklyn high school, she became deeply steeped in youth culture, observing their enthusiasm for urban contemporary fiction. Her literary insight, along with her passion for writing, prompted the creation of the Telham Park series. Jennifer resides in New Jersey.